# Murder at the Windsor Club

Stephen E. Stanley

# Murder at the Winsor Club

ISBN-10:  1470109719
ISBN-13:  978-1470109714

Printed in the United States of America.

Stonefield Publishing 2012

*Also by Stephen E. Stanley*

**A MIDCOAST MURDER**
*A Jesse Ashworth Mystery*

**MURDER IN THE CHOIR ROOM**
*A Jesse Ashworth Mystery*

**THE BIG BOYS DETECTIVE AGENCY**
*A Jesse Ashworth Mystery*

**JIGSAW ISLAND**
*A novel of Maine*

**MUDER ON MT. ROYAL**
*A Jesse Ashworth Mystery*

**COASTAL MAINE COOKING**
*The Jesses Ashworth Cook Book*

## Author's Note:

This book is a work of fiction. All characters, names, institutions, and situations depicted in the book are the product of my imagination and not based on any persons living or dead. Anyone who thinks he or she is depicted in the book is most likely delusional and should be institutionalized.

Stonefield Publishing
Portland, Maine
StonefieldPublishing@gmail.com

Author's Web page: http://stephenestanley.com/

I would like to thank Stonefield Publishing for taking a chance on an unknown writer. Small publishers such as Stonefield do not have the resources that big publishing companies have and do not have a full-time staff of copyreaders. Any typos or omissions are strictly my own. I'm a writer, not a typist. Anyone looking for editorial perfection should stick to the big publishers and pay accordingly.

I would also like to thank my partner Raymond Brooks for his continued support and dog sitting skills.

Stephen E. Stanley 2012

# Murder at the Windsor Club

## Stephen E. Stanley

## Cast of Characters

**Jeremy Dance**—Jeremy is young, rich, and very good at restoring lost things.

**Judy Hogarth**—Jeremy's best friend and a young Back Bay socialite.

**Robert Williams**—an heir to a popular canned meat business, Rob prefers to live simply as a homicide detective for the Boston Police.

**Roscoe Jackson**—a gentleman of color, Roscoe is Jeremy's right hand man.

**Velda Dance**—Jeremy's twin sister and an artist in her own right.

**Lyle Compton**—Manger of the Windsor Club.

**Bishop Angus Campbell**—a fund raiser for the Episcopal Diocese.

**Bishop Colin Anderson**—the head of the Boston diocese.

**Archdeacon Peter Ramsey**—Bishop Anderson's assistant.

**Canon Tim Black**—manger of the Boston diocese.

**Sister Mary**—the Mother Superior of the Order of St. Columba.

**Ruth Stone**—lost her son in the war and believes she can contact him through a medium.

**Ramon Decamp**—a spiritual medium who has a loyal following.

**Betty Bronson**—Ramon Decamp's "assistant."

**Myra Pennington**—society columnist for the *Boston Post*.

**Donna Jefferson**—hires Jeremy to investigate a possible fraud.

**Marjorie Barrymore**—a seventeen year old young lady who goes missing.

**Jane Chambers**—she has lost something of sentimental value.

**Tommy Beckford**—appears interested in Velda.

**Agnes Parker**—a key witness, but is she reliable?

**Henry Stanton**—head curator of the Langley Museum.

**Jimmy Kirk**—comes to work for the Dance household.

*Boston is an oasis in the desert, a place where the larger proportion of people are loving, rational and happy.*
**--Julia Ward Howe**

## Chapter 1

It was New Year's Day 1936 and my assistant Roscoe was busy outside polishing the little brass plaque on my front door. The plaque simply read: *Jeremy Dance, Restorations*. I didn't have to advertise my business as word of mouth seemed to suffice. Beacon Hill people like to keep secrets and always pay well to keep their private business quiet. Anyway, every New Year's Roscoe goes through the house and cleans from top to bottom. He believes that cleaning the house clears out the old year's phantoms and makes way for the new. I'm not sure why he bothers as we have a woman who comes in during the week to do for us.

It's an indictment against society that a man like Roscoe Jackson, a graduate of Tuskegee, could only find work as a railroad porter and chef. Whenever I railed against the injustice of it, Roscoe would just look at me and say, "We all have our parts to play." That's Roscoe, always cool and level-headed.

I first met Roscoe several years ago when he was the chef at a small Boston restaurant called Chappy's. The food was so special that one night, when I was far from sober, I sent for the chef to praise his skill and offer a rather generous tip.

1

That's how we met. After the stock market crash businesses began to go bankrupt, but the restaurant held on for a few years. But one day two years ago, I went to the restaurant for dinner with a friend and found only a sign on the door that said "closed."

At the time I had just bought a Beacon Hill townhouse for a steal and was in the process of setting up a household. It took me several days of inquiries, but I finally tracked Roscoe down to a rooming house in a rundown neighborhood of Boston. As I turned up the street I realized I was the only white person in sight. I boldly walked up to the dilapidated row house and rang the buzzer. The rooming house smelled of cooked cabbage and urine, and the interior was lit with only a single, dim bulb in the hallway.

An old lady in a dirty torn housecoat yelled up the stairs, "Jackson, some white guy to see you." I heard several doors open a saw dark eyes peering out at me. I heard steps on the stairs and then Roscoe appeared.

"Mr. Dance, what are you doing here?"

"I've come to offer you a job."

"I'll take it."

"But I haven't told you what it is."

"Don't care. I'll take it."

"It's a live-in position."

"Let's go."

"Don't you want to pack up your things?"

"Nothing to pack up. Let's go."

There was a maid's bedroom off my kitchen. It had a small bathroom attached, and it was furnished with a bed, bureau, an easy chair, and a radio. It was modest, but when I showed it to Roscoe you would have thought it was a suite at the Ritz. And that's how Roscoe Jackson became my cook, valet, and personal secretary.

How I ended up in Boston is a different story. I'm from a well-known Philadelphia family who shall remain nameless, and Dance is a family name on my mother's less famous Boston side. My father bought me off on the condition that I move away and stay away. It had something to do with a scandal with an army officer and former school mate and some incriminating photographs. I was glad to leave Philadelphia, but I made the family pay dearly for my disappearance.

"Lady to see you, Mr. Jeremy."

"Send her in, Roscoe."

Roscoe admitted a young woman about twenty-five years of age. I could tell by the way she dressed that she was one of the Boston elite. I didn't see a wedding ring.

"Hello. I'm Jeremy Dance, How can I help you?" I said as I stood.

"Mr. Dance. I was given your name by a friend of mine. I understand you can accomplish certain results discretely."

"Please have a seat Miss...?" I indicated a chair opposite mine by the fire.

"Jane Chambers." She sat down. Roscoe came in with a pot of coffee and two cups.

"Coffee Miss Chambers?"

"Yes, thank you. Just black." I passed her the coffee and added cream to my own. I gave her a chance to drink before I got to the question. The name Chambers rang a bell. It was the name of a prominent Boston area banking family.

"What brings you out on such a cold day, Miss Chambers?"

"I've lost a ruby brooch, Mr. Dance, and I'd want to get it back."

"When you say lost, what do you mean?"

"I think it's been stolen."

"Is it insured?"

"Yes, but it was given to me by my fiancé, and it has sentimental value."

"Well then, you better tell me the story," I suggested and sat back to listen.

"My fiancé David gave me the ruby brooch for Christmas. A few days later it was missing from my jewelry box."

"Can you describe it for me?"

"It's fairly simple. It has a one carat red ruby surrounded by three entwined gold strands. The whole thing is about three and a half inches in height."

"So it's not really remarkable at all?"

"No, it's very simple."

"Do you have any idea of the value?"

"My fiancé is not wealthy, and I'd guess that he spent maybe fifty dollars all together."

"What makes you guess that?" I asked.

"We set a limit on the cost of our presents to each other. We're saving up for our wedding."

I nodded. Roscoe appeared with a tray of finger sandwiches and placed them on the table. Jane Chambers and I took a few moments to sample the sandwiches before we got back to business.

"Tell me about your household."

"Well it's me and my older sister Barbara, my brother Daniel, and my parents."

"Your father is Jeffrey Chambers, the banker?"

"Yes. Do you know him?"

"We've met," I answered. "Household staff?"

"We have a couple. They've been with us since before I was born. I'm sure they weren't involved."

"Give me their names." She told me and I wrote them down.

"Has anything else gone missing?" I asked.

"No. That's why this is so strange."

"I'll do my best to find the broach."

"Thank you. What are you going to charge me?"

"I get ten dollars an hour plus expenses. However as I know your father I'm cutting the payment in half."

"Thank you, Mr. Dance."

"Consider it an early wedding present."

Jane Chambers left and I reached for my notebook to write down the information she gave me. Roscoe came into the room and cleared away the tray. Soon he reappeared.

"Miss Hogarth to see you sir." Judy Hogarth came breezing into the room and flopped down opposite me by the fireplace. I took one look at her.

"Roscoe, we could use two martinis, please."

"Make one for yourself, too Roscoe. You're family," offered Judy.

Roscoe looked at me and I nodded. He soon returned with three drinks and placed them on the tea table.

"Trouble with your lovely girlfriend?"

"We broke up. She said she couldn't live like this. It wasn't right." I nodded to Roscoe to have a seat.

Judy Hogarth and I are best friends. Whenever we need a date for appearance sake we cover for each other. Most people assume that we are a couple. We kept our private lives discrete.

"I've been there," said Roscoe. "There are plenty more nice women out there for you." Roscoe was, as we say, 'in the life,' as both Judy and I were. Many times I've seen men exiting out the back door of my house in the early morning hours.

"Never mind," I said. "It's New Year's Day. We get a fresh start. I've got plenty of booze and Roscoe will make us a nice dinner."

"Thanks, Jeremy," said Judy, trying to stifle a sob.

"In fact I just got a new case. I could use your help. Get your mind off that ungrateful wench."

"That," she said wiping the tears out of her eyes, "would be wonderful."

The three of us were sitting in the kitchen enjoying a wonderful roast beef dinner that Roscoe had prepared. My Beacon Hill neighbors would be horrified to learn that I was not only eating in the kitchen, but also sitting down to dinner with a "servant." They would be more horrified by some of my other activities as well, but that wasn't my problem. The kitchen was Roscoe's domain, and I felt honored to be his guest, as did Judy. To hell with the class system.

"So what is this job you have for us, Mr. Jeremy," asked Roscoe.

"It's a missing piece of jewelry. It has great sentimental value, but little else."

"Some rich bitch, I bet," sighed Judy.

"If I recall correctly," I said, "you are also a rich bitch."

"So are you sweetie," she smiled at me. Roscoe cleared his throat.

"Judy, I need you to go to the pawn shops along Arlington Street and see if you can find the brooch." I gave her a brief description of the bauble.

"And Roscoe, I need you to check with your contacts and see what you can learn about the Chamber's household."

"Yes, Mr. Jeremy."

"And if I'm not mistaken," I added, "We could use another round of drinks."

Judy and I retired to the living room after dinner to enjoy a nice glass of port. Somewhere off in the house I heard the phone ringing and shortly after Roscoe came into the room.

"Telephone for you, Mr. Jeremy."

"Take a message, Roscoe." I was too comfortable to move.

"It's Mr. Compton from the Windsor Club. He said it was an emergency." Lyle Compton was the manager of the Windsor Club, one of the most exclusive and private men's club in Boston.

"Thank you, Roscoe. Tell him I'll be with him shortly." I took one more sip of the port, heaved myself out of the easy chair, and made my way into the study.

"Happy New Year, Lyle. What can I do for you?"

"Mr. Dance, we have a situation here. It's an emergency and we need your help."

"What kind of an emergency?" I asked.

"I'd rather not say over the phone. Could you please come? It's most important."

"I'll be over as soon as I can," I sighed. It was New Year's Day and the temperature was hovering around ten degrees.

Roscoe has a six sense about him and already had the sixteen cylinder yellow Cadillac 452-D waiting for me in front of the house as soon as I got into my heavy coat. Roscoe is always happy to take the wheel whenever 1 don't feel like driving.

"Sorry Judy. Something's come up. It's late and cold outside, so please stay the night. The guest room is all made up."

"Be careful, Jeremy."

"I'm always careful."

I hopped in the front seat with Roscoe as he drove carefully through the Boston streets. The Windsor Club was on outer Commonwealth Avenue. Here and there along the way we saw groups of party goers staggering along the streets.

"Seems to be a lot of celebrating going on," observed Roscoe.

"Times have improved since Mr. Roosevelt took charge."

"Don't let your fancy Beacon Hill friends hear you say that."

"They may be my peers," I said, "but they definitely aren't my friends. And my family members are staunch republicans, and you know how I feel about them."

"The republicans or your family?"

"Both as it turns out."

Roscoe dropped me off at the front door while he went to park the car. One of the things I like about the Winsor club is that they have a lounge for the drivers and assistants of the members. It was quite comfortable with easy chairs and their own bar.

When I say that the Windsor Club is an exclusive club, I really mean that there are strict requirements for membership. First of all you have to have lots of money. It also helps if you come from old money. Second of all you must be absolutely discrete and open minded. The club was a place to be with other like-minded men and be far away from wives, mothers, sisters, and all women in their many roles. In other words the members preferred the company of men to that of women, if you understand my meaning.

Discretion is, of course, the foremost requirement as the membership includes Boston politicians, famous actors, bishops, lawyers, doctors, and other community leaders.

"Thank God you're here, Jeremy," said Lyle Compton as I stepped into the reception area. "Come with me. There's been an accident."

"Accident?" Lyle didn't answer but took me through to the back entrance of the kitchen and out into the alley. Then he pointed to a heap of clothing lying in the shadows.

"The chef found him there when he went outside for a smoke."

I walked up to the heap for a closer look. I knelt down, pulled out my lighter, and held the flame close to the face. The first thing I saw was a glint of gold. Looking down I saw a pectoral cross. I picked up a wrist and checked for a pulse. There wasn't any.

"It's Bishop Campbell," I said as I held the flame up to the face. I heard Lyle's quick intake of breath. My guess was he hadn't realized that the corpse was that of a member of the club. "His head has been bashed in."

"Oh, my God!" screamed Lyle.

"Calm down, Lyle," I replied. "We've a lot to do and panic isn't going to help."

"What are we going to do? Oh my God, this is awful."

"First of all, you need to call the police and ask for Lieutenant Williams. This is murder. The second thing we have to do is protect the bishop's reputation and the reputation of the club. And we have to find out who murdered the bishop, because in truth, all of us could be in danger."

"What do you need me to do?"

"Get me a list of everyone in the club tonight, and then send them home. We don't need the police interviewing our members. The chef found the body, so he'll need to talk to the police. Call Andy Goodwin. He's our club's attorney. Leave the police to me."

Lieutenant Robert Williams and I were classmates at Andover back in your youth. Unlike me his family hadn't quite disowned him. Rob wanted to be a cop and his father wanted him to take over the canned meat business. Rob had lots of family money, but he preferred living modestly. I waited in the alley by the body until Rob pulled up in his green Chevrolet coupe.

"Jeremy, what the hell?" said Rob as he stepped out of the car. Rob Williams had the smoldering good looks that could drive men to their knees.

"Bishop Campbell. Retired bishop of the Episcopal Church from the Midwest berretta belt. His head's been bashed in."

"How long?"

"The chef next door stepped out into the alley to have a smoke and stumbled over the body around ten this evening.

"I'll have to talk to him." Rob looked around the alley. "This is the back of the Windsor Club isn't it?"

"Yes, and you know that we can't afford a scandal. You know who the members are?"

"I know who some of them are, yes." Rob was not a member of the club, but he was often a guest of mine and had a good idea of what he was dealing with.

"I'm guessing," I said thinking quickly, "that he must have been on his way to dinner at Gibby's restaurant over there on the corner."

"He must have been taking a shortcut through the alley," suggested Rob.

"That's as good a story as any."

"A bishop murdered in Boston. The public are going to be screaming for justice. There has already been a campaign by *The Boston Post* complaining about the rise in crime and how the police are just being lazy."

"We need to keep this as quiet as possible and find the murderer," I said. "I'll make a few calls and see what I can do."

"I suppose," sighed Rob, "the the good bishop here didn't just fall and split his head open?"

"From the extent and position of the wound, I'd say no. However, it will make a good cover story until we can look further."

"You'll help?"

"Of course," I answered. "What are friends for?"

# Chapter 2

It was ten in the morning before Judy emerged from the guest room. Roscoe had taken her a tray earlier and now she entered the study where I was making a few phone calls. Roscoe came in with a fresh pot of coffee on a silver tray.

"Roscoe, be sure to get the evening paper today, would you?"

"Yes, sir.

"And take the rest of the day off. I need you to contact some of your less savory acquaintances and see if we can track down Miss Chambers's missing jewelry. Judy, I want you to start looking in the pawn shops. Give them a sense of the type of jewelry you're looking for and see if anyone offers you something."

"If they do?"

"Don't ask any questions, just buy it. I'll do the follow up."

"You suspect something, don't you?" asked Roscoe."

"Yes, Mr. Jackson, I have a theory."

"So where did you two go off to last night?" asked Judy as she poured out a cup of coffee.

I motioned her to sit down and filled her in on what had transpired at the Windsor Club.

"So the bishop was murdered?"

"Yes, it seems that way, but we don't know why or by whom."

"How long can you pass it off as an accident?"

"Probably not as long as we'd like."

Before I could elaborate further, the door bell rang and Roscoe went to answer it. Shortly after Roscoe returned.

"Three gentlemen to see you Mr. Jeremy. I put them in the front parlor."

"Thank you Roscoe. Offer them some coffee and then you can take the car." I thought Roscoe would faint with joy to get the car to himself. "What type of gentlemen are they?"

"Churchy types."

"Good lord," exclaimed Judy.

"Exactly," I responded.

The three gentlemen were standing in the parlor with their coffee cups looking very ill at ease. All three were well into middle age and overweight. One of them had on a purple shirt with a white collar and a large gold cross. I recognized him as a bishop. The second and taller man was dressed in the black of a priest, and the third and younger of the three was wearing a navy pin-stripe suit. All three snapped to attention when I entered the room.

"Good morning gentlemen," I said. "Please have a seat and tell me how I can help you. I'm Jeremy Dance."

"I'm Colin Anderson," said the bishop.

"Happy to meet you, your grace," I said falling back on my high church Episcopal upbringing.

"This is my assistant, Archdeacon Peter Ramsey," he said pointing to the priest. And this is our diocesan manager, Canon Tim Black." We shook hands all around and then I motioned the guests to the offered seats.

"We understand," said Bishop Anderson, "that you are a gentleman of discretion."

"I believe that is my reputation," I responded.

"We also understand that you are familiar with our recent tragedy," began the Archdeacon.

"If you mean the murder of Bishop Campbell, yes I am. Let's not beat around the bush gentlemen. People seek me out for a reason." All three of them seemed suddenly interested in studying the pattern of the oriental rug on the floor.

"Very well then" said Tim Black. "We want to avoid any scandal that might reflect negatively on the church. We'd like you to look into the unpleasantness surrounding the recent passing of Bishop Campbell and devise a way to keep the press from blowing this out of proportion."

"I see," I said. "I'd be happy to help." I could see immediately a look of relief wash across their faces. Without missing a beat Tim Black reached into his suit pocket and unfolded a check and passed it to me.

"Would this be sufficient for a retainer?"

I looked at the check. "Yes, this will do."

"And what is your standard fee?"

I gave them the figure and then added, "Of course, as an Episcopalian, I'd be happy to offer a special price." They agreed to the price, and we shook hands all around. I showed them to the door and then went back to the study to join Judy.

"What was that all about?" she asked as I poured more coffee in my cup and sat down.

I gave her the short version, and she rolled her eyes.

"You lead a very interesting life, Jeremy."

"It does seem that way," I answered. "Now off you go to the pawn shops."

Jeremiah Morse stood in front of me twisting his chef's hat in his hands. The Windsor Club's kitchen was large and well appointed and extremely clean. The chef was a shy man, and he had difficulty looking me in the eyes.

"Tell me exactly what you saw when you stepped out into the alley."

"I've already told the police."

"And I know that as a loyal club employee, you gave them as little as possible. I'm representing the club, so you need to tell me everything."

"I had just stepped out for a smoke and…"

17

"Stop right there," I said. Jeremiah looked startled. "You don't smoke. I can smell a smoker a mile away. There's no smoke smell on you and there are no stains on your fingers. You went out into the alley to meet someone, didn't you?"

Jeremiah just nodded and looked at the floor.

"I know you fear for your job, but I'm not here to get you fired. I just need to know who you were meeting."

"I wasn't meeting anyone," he said. I looked at him and caught his eye. "I mean, sometimes people hang out in the alley. I sometimes take a break and step outside and talk to them."

"What do you mean people hang out in the alley?"

"Sometimes men come here to sell things. The alley is dark, and the police don't come around often. It's well known that if you're in the market for a watch, or a necklace, or something, then you might just find it here."

"In other words," I said. "guys come here to sell stolen goods."

"No one ever said they were stolen."

"I'm sure they didn't," I agreed. "What else happens here?" I knew from experience that whenever one type of crime flourished that there was bound to be more.

"Sometimes ladies come here to…" Jeremiah stopped to look for the right words.

"Make some cash?" I added. He just nodded. "Boys too?" He nodded again. "I see." My question was which vice was the good bishop looking for when he was murdered. It was none of my business as to why Jeremiah was there, but I did need to ask more questions.

"So you stepped outside into the alley. Was there anyone else there?"

"No one that I saw."

"Did you hear something?"

"I heard what sounded like someone kicking a trash can."

"Where did the sound come from?"

"It sounded like it was coming around the corner."

"I think you better show me."

Chef Jeremiah grabbed his overcoat and we stepped out into the alley. A cold wind greeted us as the wind whipped through the narrow alley. The alley was wide enough maybe for one automobile to travel. The alley was almost a block long and the buildings on either side had rear doors onto the alley.

"The noise came from over there," he said pointing to a small passage between two buildings." There were smaller alleys leading off from the main back alley. They were passages between the buildings that were just big enough for foot traffic. No wonder this alley was well-known for secret activities. It was dark and secluded and it had many little escape routes where one could hide.

"When did you see the body?"

"The body was to the left of the door, as you know." I stepped out and looked around. At first I didn't see him, but when I turned around to go back inside I saw what looked like feet sticking out from behind the garbage cans."

"When I saw the body there were no trash cans," I said.

"I moved them to the other side of the alley, before anyone got here."

"Who told you to do that?"

"Mr. Compton."

"Of course," I said. "Thanks Jeremiah, and for the record, we never had this conversation." He just nodded and walked back to his kitchen.

## Chapter 3

January was bitter cold, and I tried to stay inside as much as possible. Looking out the window of my second floor study I could see much of Beacon Hill. The sun was out and everything looked frosty and cold in the morning. I was on my second cup of coffee when Judy Hogarth sauntered in. She was wearing stylish black boots and was wrapped up in a fur coat. Right behind her was Roscoe. He took her hat and coat and disappeared. Judy took a seat in the red chair in front of my desk. She reached into her purse and pulled out a small bundle wrapped up in a white handkerchief. Roscoe reappeared with another cup of coffee and set it down for Judy.

"What have you got there Judy?" I asked, though I had a pretty good idea what it was.

"I think," she said, unwrapping the bundle, "you are looking for this."

"That's the one," I said looking at the brooch. "Where did you find it?"

"It was in a pawn shop over in Jamaica Plain."

"How much did you pay for it?"

"Twenty dollars."

I opened my desk drawer and pulled out my checkbook and wrote her a check for the amount. "Good job."

"None of my leads worked out," said Roscoe.

"I have a feeling this wasn't a professional job. After lunch, Roscoe, I think we need to take a ride to Jamaica Plain."

"Yes sir."

Roscoe had the car warmed up before Judy and I slipped into the back seat. We pulled the car rug over our legs to keep out the cold that the car's heater was having a hard time combating.

"I think all the heat is in the front seat, Roscoe."

"It's nice and toasty up here, Mr. Jeremy."

"You're fired!" I laughed.

"You fire me now, there won't be any dinner."

"Never mind then." Roscoe pulled onto Huntington Avenue and past the museum and out toward the less congested parts of the city. Judy and I watched the sights of the city slip by as we sat in companionable silence.

"How are you doing?" I finally asked.

"Not great," she sighed. "I don't like being dumped."

"No one does."

"No one ever dumps you, Jeremy."

"No, they just move away, or get a job somewhere, or decide to marry for appearances."

"They're all assholes, then."

"I think," I said. "it's time for a dinner party."

"Oh, Jeremy, that's a great idea."

"I'll do some recruiting and see what I come up with."

Roscoe parked the car in front of the pawn shop. The irony of a well-dressed, upper-class couple stepping out of the new Cadillac, and entering a pawn shop wasn't lost on us. It wasn't lost on the proprietor either.

"What can I do for you?" asked the middle-aged clerk. He had a red face and was bald and bore a striking resemblance to a famous character actor of the moving pictures.

"My fiancée, Miss Hogarth, purchased a ruby brooch here yesterday." Judy gave me a kick behind the counter when I said fiancée.

"Oh, yes, I remember."

"It's a really nice piece, I was just wondering if you could give us a little background on the piece. For instance, who left it here?"

"I really can't discuss my clients business. You understand."

"Maybe this will loosen your lips,' I answered passing him a ten dollar bill.

"I'm sorry, I really can't say," he said reaching under the counter for his record book. "I need to go into the back room for a few minutes. Please don't look at my records." He opened the book, turned it toward me, and walked out of the room.

I ran my finger down the page until I came to the line I was looking for. I read the name. "I think we're done here."

Jane Chambers lived with her family in a large Back Bay townhouse on Newbury Street. I had called ahead and Jane answered the door and ushered me into a small reception room. The room was ornately furnished in a style that had gone out of favor at the turn of the century, but the Victorian furnishings were pretty standard for the Back Bay.

"You found my brooch?"

"Yes," I answered. I retrieved it from my pocket and handed it to her. She reached out for it and turned it over in her hand.

"I can't thank you enough," she said. "This means the world to me."

"It's what you paid me to do, Miss Chambers."

"Where did you find it?"

"I'm going to give you some advice. Sometimes it's best not to know certain things."

"But I need to know." She looked at me intently

"Very well, then," I sighed. "It was found in a pawn shop in Jamaica Plain."

"A pawn shop? So someone stole it and pawned it. How much did they pawn it for?"

"Five dollars."

"Five dollars, but it's worth sixty!"

"Actually, Miss Chambers, it's worth well over a hundred dollars according to the appraisal. It looks like your fiancé has very good taste."

"Oh, that wonderful man! He can't afford something that expensive."

"It's love, Miss Chambers. You are a lucky woman." I could see the wheels turning in her head.

"Do you know who pawned it?"

"Yes, but I think it would be best to forget about it."

"I want to know."

"The name on the register was Barbara Chambers."

"My sister? Why?" I could tell she was shocked.

"You'll have to ask her," I said. "But I suspect that she is envious of your happiness."

"You can believe that I'll be talking with her." Jane Chambers took out a check book and paid the bills. "I can trust you to be discrete?"

"Of course, that's why people hire me."

Roscoe dropped me off at the Windsor Club. I was meeting Lieutenant Robert Williams for lunch, and the Windsor Club prided itself on its good food. Lyle Compton was waiting for me at the check-in desk.

"Could I have a moment with you Mr. Dance?'

"Of course Lyle, what is it?" He motioned me into his office and shut the door.

"We are, of course, most anxious about the unpleasantness of the other night."

25

"If by unpleasantness, you mean the bashing in of the bishop's head, I think you should be concerned."

"We can't afford a scandal."

"Forget the scandal, Lyle. You need to think about the safety of all the members. There was a murder in the back alley of the club. Who's to say there won't be another death?"

I watched as the color drained from Lyle's face. I was afraid he would faint. I could tell he hadn't thought of that.

"Oh, my god!" he exclaimed. I could see the seriousness of the situation was finally sinking in.

"The church has hired me to look into the bishop's death. I'm having lunch with the lead police investigator, who is a good friend of mine. I plan to solve the murder discretely. I suggest you hire some additional security just as a precaution."

"Yes, I think we should."

"Now if you'll excuse me, I have a lunch date."

# Chapter 4

The snow had begun falling as I looked out of the window of the club's dining room The scene outside looked very wintery and there was a blue cast to everything outside. The waiter brought my cocktail just as Rob Williams, immaculately dressed in a wool suit, was escorted to my table by the head waiter.

"Sorry to be late, but I had to clear up some paperwork on my desk."

"I understand, though why you want to be a cop escapes me?"

"It's much more interesting than the family business. I'm sure you feel the same way."

"My family's business, as far as I can tell, is being pompous and rich." The waiter came over and we ordered lunch.

"This is supposed to be the beginning of a major snow storm," observed Rob as he looked out the window at the deepening snow.

"I think we need to take a vacation and go sailing in the Caribbean."

"The last time we went sailing," Rob reminded me, "your family disowned you."

"And you almost got kicked out of the army," I added.

"So a photographer took pictures of us sailing in the nude, big deal!"

"My family wasn't amused by the photos at all," I laughed.

"I thought we looked wonderful in those shots," said Rob.

"Talk about sunburn!" I said. We both laughed at the memory.

"I have some time I can take off in February. We should go to Florida."

"I'll have Roscoe arrange it," I said. Our lunch arrived. Rob wasn't drinking because he had to go back on duty, but I ordered another cocktail.

"Any leads on the case?" I asked, getting to the business that brought us here.

"Yes, and you?"

"Yes," I said and then told him about what I learned from the chef.

"You think the bishop was in the alley to buy stolen goods or worse?"

"Hard to say," I answered. "The bishop was a frequent patron of the club, so he may have just stepped outside to get some air, or he may have really been going to Gibby's for dinner.

"Or to get away from some of those tedious members who were probably telling one of their tedious stories."

"I see you've noticed the caliber of some of the members."

"If I hear John Huntington's stories about India one more time, I might be tempted to bash in my own brains."

"Your turn," I said to Rob.

"All I have so far is some background information. Bishop Campbell was formerly from the Diocese of Fond du Lac in Wisconsin. He's been retired in this area for ten years, and is seventy-two years of age. He occasionally helps out at local churches and is a member of the Boston cathedral. He was unmarried and the only living relative is a sister in Eau Clair, Wisconsin. We contacted her and she was unaware of any reason someone would have to kill him."

"Does she know it was murder?"

"We only said we are looking at all possibilities." We stopped briefly while the waiter refilled our water glasses.

"I have a plan," I said after the waiter left.

"I'm not going to like this am I?"

"Most likely not," and then I outlined my plan.

"It might work, but is does have dangers. I'm going with you," said Rob. "But looking at how much snow has fallen in the last hour, I think we'll have to wait a few days."

"Why don't you stay at my house tonight after you get off work? That way you won't have to trudge out into the hinterlands in the snow."

"Staying with you," said Rob with a twinkle in his eye, "has its own dangers."

Roscoe served us breakfast in the parlor as Rob and I listened to the radio. The gentle snow of yesterday afternoon had turned into a major blizzard that had all but crippled the city of Boston. The snow had fallen so fast the work crews had been unable to clear the trolley lines. Any thoughts of investigation were put on hold. The storm was expected to be a two day event and then storm cleanup would take several days more.

"I'm due back on duty at noon," Rob said after the weather forecast.

"Explain to me again why you like being a cop," I remarked as I looked out at the blizzard.

"It's much more exciting than working in the office at a canned meat factory."

"But it's your family's factory."

"You want to work at your family business?"

"God, no! Okay, I see your point. How's your relationship with them?"

"They've come around, though they don't understand that I want to live simply, like a cop. And they never were upset by those photos."

"No reason to be, my family paid the blackmail and bought the photos, negatives and all."

"It was your family that had a fit."

"My family is all about show, and nothing about substance."

"Except your sister."

"That's true," I agreed. "Velda is a free spirit."

"What's new with her?"

"Last time I heard from her she was in Berlin setting up her art studio."

"How does your father feel about her being an artist?"

"She's a girl, so he doesn't take her seriously. He and my stepmother are just waiting for her to tire of her "hobby," and they have a whole list of eligible men for her to marry."

"Your family makes mine look good," said Rob and I don't think he was joking.

"I need to go to the store," said Roscoe as he entered the room. "You gentlemen need anything before I go?"

"Thank you, Roscoe; I think we'll be okay."

"Be safe out there, Mr. Jackson," added Rob.

"You too, Mr. Williams," said Roscoe as he shot Rob a smile.

"He's a gem," said Rob after Roscoe's exit.

"He manages this house and my business with skill, and me, too, come to think of it."

The hardest part of planning a dinner party was choosing the guests. All I really had to do was tell Roscoe how many guests I invited, and it would all be taken care of. The challenging part would be finding a suitable companion for Judy Hogarth. I knew a good number of independent women, but calling them up and asking if they had lesbian tendencies was probably not a good idea, so I did what any good Bostonian would do, I called up the local Beacon Hill gossip and made a short list up based on rumor and innuendo.

Unlike my stepmother planning a dinner party, I didn't have to worry about having an equal number of men and women. My list would be mostly younger men, a few older women who were open minded and interesting, and a couple of possible friends for Judy.

For his part Roscoe made it clear that we should hire some additional help for him at the party. From experience I knew that this "help" would be composed of good-looking, younger men.

"You think you can find some help?" I asked him.

"Like shooting fish in a barrel," he answered. I decided to let that one go by without comment.

"I suppose they'll need serving attire?"

"Something simple, I think, would be fine. How formal is this going to be?" asked Roscoe.

"Semi-formal. White dinner jackets for the men, evening gowns for the women."

"And the menu?"

"I leave that up to you, Mr. Jackson. I trust your judgment completely."

## Chapter 5

The blizzard lasted for two days and the cleanup took two more. I was anxious to start looking into the death of the bishop, but I knew it would be useless until the weather settled down. The bitter cold, coupled with the wind, meant that my plans would be on hold until warmer weather settled in Boston. I suppose it didn't matter, the bishop would be just as dead a week from now. My hope was that any clues I could garner wouldn't disappear.

I must have been daydreaming because the next thing I knew there was a knock on the office door, and Roscoe admitted a young lady in a fur coat.

"This is Miss Jefferson," said Roscoe.

"Have a seat Miss Jefferson," I said. "Would you like something to drink?"

"No thank you. Your boy already offered me something." I saw Roscoe stiffen at the word "boy."

"I can assure you, Miss Jefferson, that my assistant Mr. Jackson hasn't been a boy for several decades." I motioned Roscoe to sit down.

"I'm sorry; I didn't mean to offend you, Mr. Jackson." The apology won her a few points.

"What can I do for you, Miss Jefferson?"

"Please call me Donna. It's my aunt Ruth Stone. She's very rich, but I'm afraid she's being taken in by a medium."

"I think you better tell me the whole story," I said. "Mr. Jackson will take down some notes."

"I should give you some background first. My parents died several years ago, and I've been living with my aunt, my mother's sister. She's the only family I have. My aunt has a lot of money and I'm afraid that this medium is going to rob her."

"So you stand to inherit her money when she dies? I'm not passing judgment, Miss Jefferson, just trying to clarify the situation."

"That's true, Mr. Dance, but I'm concerned that she may be cheated out of her fortune by a fraud."

"I see. Go on."

"About two months ago my aunt went to see this medium. He says he is Professor Ramon Decamp, and he claims he can contact the dead. He told my aunt that he could contact her dead son David, and her late husband Herbert."

"What made your aunt think that he could contact them?"

"He was able to describe them in detail and give facts about their lives. David died in the war, and Ramon gave her the details of his death. The details matched the information she received from the army."

"Was there any way he could have gathered the information?"

"It would take a little digging, but I think he could have researched the details."

"What makes you think that he's after her fortune?"

"The visits keep becoming more frequent. Ramon says that they have an important message for her, but the connection to the other world is not clear. Every time he tries to contact the dead, the spirits become weak, so he has to keep scheduling another reading. He's charging her money for each séance."

"I'm in the wrong business," muttered Roscoe.

"What would you like me to do, Miss Jefferson?"

"I'd like you to prove that this Professor Ramon person is a fraud and get him away from my aunt. I think she's in danger from this guy. And I'd like to keep this private. I don't want anyone to think my aunt is crazy. I understand your services aren't cheap." She reached into her handbag and pulled out a check. "Will this be enough of a retainer?"

"This should cover the initial investigation," I said looking at the amount of the check. "I'll let you know if there will be any additional charges."

"Thank you Mr. Dance," and then she added, "And Mr. Jackson."

"I think we need to visit this Ramon," I said to Roscoe after she left.

Judy Hogarth was dressed to the nines when I picked her up for dinner. We were dining at the Ritz. It was a Thursday night and the elite of Boston would be in attendance. Both Judy and I knew most of the regulars, and we exchanged discrete waves and smiles as the host led us across the dining room into a quiet corner. It always helps to tip big.

"Isn't that Myra Pennington over by the window?" I asked. Myra was the society reporter for *The Boston Post*. Both Judy and I had figured prominently in her columns.

"Yes it is. I wonder who she's with." Myra was dining with a man in his sixties. I recognized him as the owner of a Lowell shoe factory, but I couldn't remember his name.

"New money," I said. "Most likely trying to get into the society pages." I was watching Judy watch Myra. Myra was an attractive and stylish woman, and, according to the Beacon Hill gossip, preferred female company. I mentally added her to my dinner party list. It was never a bad idea to invite a society columnist to a party.

"I'd love to know where she shops."

"How would you like to go on an adventure?" I asked changing the subject.

"Oh, yes that would be lovely. Where are we going?"

"We are going to visit Professor Ramon, the medium."

"Really? Why?"

"To hear from your poor dead Uncle Jack."

"I don't have a dead Uncle Jack."

"Exactly," I said.

The next day I phoned Ramon Decamp and made an appointment for my "wife" and me. The plan was for Judy and me to appear as a rich, but not too bright couple who needed to contact "Uncle Jack" for financial advice.

I rarely can handle two cases at once, but this one sounded like fun and if I was right, I could unmask this fake in no time at all and maybe save an old lady from losing her fortune.

I was still waiting for better weather to investigate the bishop's murder. The plan was for me to check out the business in the alley and see if I could discover what the bishop was looking for. The recent sub-zero temperatures made it probable that the activity in the alley would be on hold until warmer weather.

"How's the party planning coming along?" I asked Roscoe when he brought in my mid-morning coffee."

"I've got the menu worked out; all I need now is to know how many people will be attending."

"We should have all the RSVP's by tomorrow, and I can give you a final count then. Have you hired your temp staff yet?"

"I'm working on it."

"I just bet you are," I said laughing.

Judy Hogarth had on more jewelry than a Russian princess or maybe a French whore, I couldn't decide which, and she was wrapped in furs from head to foot.

"Just a little bit overdone aren't you?"

"We are supposed to be the newly wealthy. I thought a vulgar display of wealth would be in order. And your outfit is just a little over the top don't you think?"

"Is it the spats?" I asked. "Or is it the diamond stick pin?"

"At least you two don't look like elevator operators," piped up Roscoe from the driver's seat. "This here driver's uniform has more braid than a Kentucky colonel's." Judy and I looked at each other and gave Roscoe a salute he could see from the rear view mirror. He muttered something that sounded suspiciously like "white trash."

We were heading south to Braintree to have our first meeting with Ramon Decamp. I had asked Rob Williams to check Ramon for any police records, but he couldn't find anything. That didn't mean much as Ramon Decamp could be just an alias.

Roscoe pulled the car up in front of a modest home in a small suburban area of Braintree. Judy and I waited for Roscoe to jump out of the car and hold the door open for us. As we got out Roscoe gave us a look.

"Keep the car warm, Jeeves," I said.

"Yes, sir master," Roscoe said as he closed the car door just a bit too loudly.

We were met at the door by a man in his forties with thinning hair and a cheap gray suit. "Come in! It's bitter cold out there. I'm Ramon Decamp."

"Thank you for seeing us, Professor Decamp. I'm John Mills and this is my wife Violet."

"Pleased to make your acquaintance, Professor," said Judy in a high voice that sounded suspiciously like Minnie Mouse.

"Charming," said Ramon with a smile that I suspected came from a dentist's office. "Have a seat and tell me what brings you here." Ramon led us into a small parlor that was painted a dark red and had heavy curtains on the window. In the middle of the room was a round table with chairs arranged around it. On the side wall there was a large, ornately decorated wardrobe. There was a lit candle in the center of the table. We were seated in a small seating area off to one side of the room.

"It's Violet's uncle," I explained. "He was the one that left us tons of money. He was always good with money and was our adviser. We need his advice as to who should handle the money now."

"How long has he been dead?"

"Just a little over a month," replied Judy in her cartoon voice. Then she giggled like a fool.

"I see," said Ramon. "That's unfortunate. The newly dead have trouble communicating at first. It may take us several meetings before he is able to come through."

"But you will try?" I asked.

"Certainly," he replied. "However my fee is ten dollars a meeting."

"That's peanuts," I said and pulled a huge wad of bills from my pocket. I thought Ramon's eyes would bug out of his head as I peeled off two twenty dollar bills and gave them to him.

"I'm sorry," he said. "I don't have any change."

"Keep the difference. Let's just call it a good faith gift."

"Very generous, I'm sure. Now if you could just tell me a little something about your Uncle Jack. Not too much, mind you, otherwise you'll think I just used the information you gave me. How did he die?"

"He shot himself," squeaked Judy.

"Ah, such a pity. The suicides are often the hardest to reach."

"Oh no!" Judy started to cry. I thought she might be over acting.

"There, there Mrs. Mills. We'll do the best we can. I'm sure he'll come through for you if we really try."

"You think so?" she asked as she dried her tears.

"Yes, I do think he'll want to communicate, especially if he has unfinished business."

"Well," I said, "he did leave us a ton of money and no idea what to do with it."

"Ah, yes money," agreed Ramon. "The dead often realize too late that money is best given away."

"Really?" nodded Judy. "I'm sure Uncle Jack would like that."

"Let's set up the first séance for tomorrow at three," said Ramon.

"We'll be here! Thank you so much Professor Decamp," said Judy in her best flirty voice.

# Chapter 6

Ramon Decamp had his parlor all set up for the séance. There were three other participants present as well. I wasn't aware that the séance would be a group gathering, but I was excited when I learned that one of them was Ruth Stone, Donna Jefferson's aunt. Ruth was a well-dressed woman in her fifties with a trusting attitude. Now I could observe carefully the hold Ramon had over her.

The second guest was a short, bald elderly man named Bart Simmons. He was very interested in communicating with his wife. It was obvious his wife made all the decisions, and he was lost being on his own. He would be a perfect victim for Ramon.

Rounding out our little party was a gray-haired old lady. I was unable to learn who she was looking for, but I suspected that she was looking for reassurance that there was life after death. I thought we made a pretty desperate little group.

We were given a few minutes to mingle and talk while Ramon went about the room and set everything up. I also noticed that Ramon kept his ears open for and information he could glean from the group talking of their dearly departed.

Judy wasn't far behind me in figuring out what Ramon was up to. I heard her speaking to Ruth Stone. "My uncle really loved his little apple trees. Even with all his business dealings he had time to spend on his trees."

"My son loved to grow roses. He had a wonderful little garden before the war," replied Ruth Stone.

"Ladies and gentlemen," announced Ramon. "I think there may be a little delay. I don't think the energy is just right. Why don't you continue to talk while I attend to some business?"

"Monkey business, if you ask me," whispered Judy as she moved up beside me.

"Let's take a quick look around the room for a hidden microphone or speaking tube."

We carefully circled around the room, trying not to draw attention to ourselves. It was obvious that are little group knew each other and were in the habit of talking about their dearly departed. I pointed to the hot air ducts furnace ducts along the floor. "There seem to be more hot air ducts than needed for the size of this room," I whispered to Judy.

"Maybe he just likes to be warm," replied Judy.

"Sure, that's it."

Ramon entered the room, and I swear this is true; he was wearing a purple cape with a matching turban on his head.

"Okay everyone, if you would all take a seat at the table, we can begin. I feel that the spirits are strong tonight," announced Ramon as he lowered the lights and lit the single candle in the middle of the table. "Now if everyone will hold hands and concentrate, we may have some success. Remember not to speak and break up the atmosphere. For the benefit of our newcomers let me explain what's about to happen.

"We will sit holding hands. We are not to break the circle for any reason. When I call upon the spirits, it is important that we all concentrate. When I slip into a trance the spirits will use my energy to manifest. Sometimes they will speak through me, and if we are lucky they may speak with their own spirit voice."

"It's so exciting," gushed Agnes Brompton, the third of Ramon's regulars.

"Do you remember what the spirits say when you wake up?" I asked Ramon.

"Not at all, therefore it's important that you tell me everything," answered Ramon.

"Oh this is so wonderful," said Ruth in a soft voice. "I just know my boy is going to talk to me tonight."

"Be still, Mrs. Stone. The spirits need us to be quiet," warned Ramon. "Are there any spirits present? Let your presence be known." Suddenly the candle in the middle of the table flared up and went out, plunging us into darkness. Nice trick; I'd have to figure out how he did that. "No one move," warned Ramon. "The spirits are here."

Ruth Stone was next to me on my right. I could feel her grip my hand tighter, but she remained quiet.

"Whatever you do," intoned Ramon, who seemed to be changing his voice into a breathless whisper, "don't break the circle."

"Why are we whispering" I asked in a whisper.

"We don't want to upset the spirits." I thought it might take more than normal conversational tones to upset the dead.

"There's a young man here; I can feel his presence," whispered Ramon. Ruth clenched my hand even tighter and I could hear her breathing faster. Suddenly there was the smell of roses permeating the air.

"Oh," cried Ruth. "It's my David! I just know it is."

"Mother? Mother?" said a disembodied voice in what I assumed was a ghostly whisper. I had to admit the voice sounded impressive, if I believed in ghosts that is.

"Oh, David! Talk to me."

"The spirit is weak and has moved on," said Ramon.

Suddenly there was humming. It sounded like a woman. "Bart? Bart, are you there?"

"Yes, Mildred, I'm here," said the old man.

"Bart, you are no good with money. You need to find someone to trust to take care of all that money you've saved." The voice took on a nagging, shrewish tone.

"Yes, dear."

"Someone trustworthy like Professor Ramon."

"Yes, dear."

Ramon let out a gasp. "That's all for tonight. The spirits have taken much too much energy from me and I must rest." He stood up in the dark and turned on the lights. There in the middle of the table was an apple. Everyone looked at it as if they had never seen an apple before.

"What is this?" asked Ramon as he picked it up. "It must be a sign. Sometimes those on the other side will give us a sign. But what does the apple mean?"

"Oh," cried Judy in her cartoon voice. "It's Uncle Jack! He was always working on his apple trees." Truthfully I was getting a little tired of the voice.

"Perhaps," said Ramon. "We'll have to see. Shall we all meet again on Thursday night?" Everyone nodded their heads. Apparently they were used to these types of séances.

"I really have to go potty," squealed Judy.

"The facilities are at the top of the stairs." Judy was off like a shot.

"What was that all about?" I asked when we got back in the car. Roscoe had returned to pick us up.

"Well, the good professor has a woman."

"How do you know?"

"That's why I went to the bathroom. I was snooping around, and unless he uses lipstick and two toothbrushes, someone else lives there."

"You snooped around?"

"Yes, I've learned a few things from you."

"Good job," I said. "That explains the woman's spirit voice."

"And she must have been listening to our conversations through the heating ducts and then told him about Ruth's son's roses and the apple tree of Uncle Jack."

"And the smell of roses could have come up in the heating ducts, too."

"When you two get done congratulating yourselves," said Roscoe from the driver's seat, "I got some information, too."

"Okay Mr. Jackson, what do you have?"

"I saw the woman. I was parked up the street, and I saw her go in the back door."

"Did you get a good look at her?" asked Judy.

"Around twenty years of age or so, average height. Bundled up against the cold."

"Well, it looks like this is going to be easier to solve that I thought," I said. As soon as the words were out of my mouth, I knew I was probably wrong.

The night was still young and we both needed to unwind, so Roscoe dropped us off on Piedmont Street at the Cocoanut Grove for a drink.

The Grove had been a speakeasy during prohibition and was very popular. But it was clear that the place had seen better days, though lately its popularity had been gaining. I maintained, however, that Matt Bronstein was the best bartender in Boston. The bamboo furnishings and the palm trees gave the place a tropical flare that was much needed on a cold January night.

Roscoe had friends among the kitchen workers and was always happy to visit while I had a drink at the bar. Judy knocked back the first martini and signaled Matt for another.

"You're not planning to get drunk are you?"

"Hey, I just did the performance of a lifetime. I deserve a drink."

"I'm not sure about the performance of a lifetime, but I think Professor Ramon bought the act."

"Greed is a wonderful thing," Judy agreed.

"Isn't that Myra Pennington at that table in the corner?" It was hard to see in the dim light and the cigarette smoke. She was holding court with a group of young people. Judy turned to look in the direction I pointed.

"I do believe it is." Myra looked up at us and waved across the room. We waved back.

"Good grief," I said. "We'll probably be in her column this week."

"I can see it now: 'What attractive Philadelphia-born playboy was seen with a Back

Bay beauty? When are you going to propose to Miss H?'"

"I like to keep them guessing," I said. "Let's gather up roscoe and get out of here."

## Chapter 7

It was just about the right look, I thought as I looked into the mirror. Not too ratty and not too dressy.

"How do I look, Roscoe?"

"The outfit's fine, but you can't wear those shoes."

"What's wrong with the shoes?" I asked.

"Those are a rich man's shoes. If you're going to look down and out, you got to have down and out shoes."

"No one is going to look at my shoes in a dark alley."

"Those people are thieves and whores. Of course they're going to look at your shoes. Might even be worth stealing. I got some old shoes you can wear."

"Your feet are bigger than mine."

"And that ain't all," said Roscoe laughing as he left to fetch the shoes.

The weather had warmed up, and we were now in what we new Englanders call the January thaw. My plan was to hang out in the alley in back of the Windsor club and see what was happening and to see if I could get some idea of why the bishop was killed there. Rob Williams had wanted to go with me, but I thought it would be better to go alone, at least until I had a better idea of what goes on there.

I walked down to Park Street and took the subway out to Huntington Avenue to the Windsor

Club. I pulled the hat down over my eyes so I wouldn't be recognized by anyone. I slipped around the corner by Gibby's restaurant and headed into the alley. It was dark and it took a while for my eyes to adjust. No one was in sight as I walked between the buildings.

As I looked down one of the connecting passages I saw a bundled up figure. I headed in that direction. As I passed I heard a voice ask, "You got the time?"

"No, I don't have a watch," I answered. I felt it best not to pull out my watch in a dark alley with a stranger. I looked closer. The guy was probably no more than sixteen.

"That's not really what I meant."

"You should be home in bed."

"Piss off, asshole," the boy said and walked off.

"You looking to buy something?" said a voice behind me. I spun around to face a small man of about forty. I hadn't seen him in the shadows. "Got a watch you might like. I just overheard that you didn't have one."

"How much?"

"For you, five bucks." He passed me the watch. It was a pocket watch of good quality. When I looked closer I could tell it was a very expensive Swiss timepiece.

"Nice watch," I said.

"Take a closer look," he said and then lit a match so I could see it. The inscription read "To JD with love SD." I was certain that I had seen the watch before and had an idea who JD might be."

"I'll take it," I said. "Got anything more?"

"That's all I have today. Maybe I'll have more in a day or two."

I passed him the five bucks and made sure I got a look at his face.

Rob was waiting for me when I got back to the house. Roscoe had already fixed him a martini and he had one ready for me as well.

"What happened?" Rob asked as soon as I sat down and had a sip.

"I bought a watch." I took the watch out of my pocket and handed it to him.

"Very nice watch. It's illegal to receive stolen property you know."

"I have a good idea who it belongs to. If I'm right I'll return it."

"Whose do you think it is?" asked Rob after a rather long sip.

"The initials JD, I think, stand for John Davis. His wife's name is Susan. He's a member of the Windsor Club, and it stands to reason that someone could have picked his pocket going to or from the club."

"Will you two be wanting a late supper?" asked Roscoe as he entered the parlor with more ice.

"Yes Roscoe, I think so." I looked at Rob and he nodded. "Don't go to too much trouble, Roscoe."

"You're never too much trouble Mr. Jeremy," said Roscoe and then burst out laughing as he left the room.

"That is one strange bird," observed Rob.

"You don't know the half of it."

A half hour later Roscoe served us country fried steak, biscuits and gravy, mashed potatoes and turnip greens.

The alarm clock sounded, and I reached across Rob's sleeping form, turned it off, and then rolled out of bed. I looked out the bedroom window and saw a cold gray dawn on Beacon Hill and was tempted to crawl back in bed.

"What time is it?" asked a sleepy Rob.

"Almost seven o'clock."

"Shit! I have to get moving and get to the station. What are you doing today?"

"I'm returning a stolen watch and then going to a séance." I had filled Rob in about Professor Ramon last night.

"I'm always amazed," said Rob from the bathroom where he had to speak up over the sound of running water, "at how gullible people are."

"Gullibility is how my family made their fortune,' I said.

I called John Davis at his office and asked him to have lunch with me at the club. Then I called Judy and arranged to pick her up later for the séance. I headed over to the Windsor Club before lunch to have a talk with Lyle Compton. I had the feeling that the manager hadn't quite told me everything. I needed some more information because tomorrow I would have to check in with my churchy clients and give them a progress report. So far, I didn't have much to report.

The Windsor Club dining room was designed with lots of dark wood and leather, with heavy drapes at the window, shutting out the winter outside. There was a fire blazing in the fireplace and the artwork was understated. In the corner was a reproduction of Michelangelo's statue of David.

I was seated in the corner when I spotted John Davis enter the room. I stood up and we shook hands. John was mid-fifties with a full head of salt and pepper hair. He was slim and athletic, and very rich. The waiter rushed over and took our drink order.

"Good to see you, Jeremy," said John as he leaned back in his chair. "It's been too long."

"How's Bella, your daughter?" Bella Davis had run away from home at sixteen. John and his wife hired me to find her and bring her home. I was able to find her before any damage was done, and save them from a scandal.

"She's off to Vassar now. College life agrees with her."

"That's good to know." The waiter returned with our drinks and took our lunch order.

"I have a feeling you didn't invite me to lunch just to be sociable," John said.

"I have something that I think belongs to you." I took out the watch and placed it on the table. His eyes went wide, and he reached for the watch. I quickly snatched it up before he could grab it. "Not so fast. I need to know how you lost it. It's pretty expensive to be leaving around."

"I was here at the club one night last week, and when I got home the watch was gone. I thought I had dropped it here at the club, so I called, but they hadn't found it."

The waiter brought us our lunch on steaming plates and placed them before us. I had ordered pork chops and John had ordered chicken. The food at the club was quite remarkable. As soon as the waiter finished fussing over us, we continued.

"I have every reason to believe that someone picked your pocket. Most likely while you were in the back alley, and I want to know what you were doing there."

"Why?"

"I'm working on a case and I'm trying to find out what goes on in the alley. I don't care what you were doing there, but it would help to have a handle on the place. You are well off, so I don't believe you were there to buy cheap goods. Perhaps you were looking for company?" John looked genuinely shocked, so I guess that wasn't the reason.

"I don't have lots of money anymore. My business hasn't been good. I was selling some heirlooms to a guy who deals in goods."

"Was the watch one of them?"

"No, that was a gift. I couldn't sell it. I thought I had misplaced it."

"I see. Why not just go to a pawn shop?"

"I can't have people know my business is in trouble. I'll lose all my clients. They aren't going to trust me with their investments if they know I'm in trouble."

I passed John the watch and took out a note pad and wrote down a name and address. "Here's the name of an honest dealer. He's very discrete, and he'll give you a fair price."

"Thank you, Jeremy."

"And stay away from the alley. There's already been a murder."

## Chapter 8

It was Roscoe's night off, so I drove the Cadillac 452-D and picked Judy up at her parents' home in the Back Bay. Once again she was dressed up and bejeweled, and gave the impression of having more money that good taste.

"This is going to be fun," said Judy as she slid into the passenger-side front seat. "Do you think we'll hear from Uncle Jack tonight?"

"There is no Uncle Jack," I reminded her.

"Maybe there's an Uncle Jack we don't know about."

"I'm sure we'll have to pay for a few more sessions before Uncle Jack can make it through the veil."

"No doubt," she agreed. "How's the murder case going?"

"I'm gathering information, and I think I've made a start. According to Rob the police are quite willing to go with the accidental death theory. Otherwise there would be an outcry that there was an unsolved murder."

"How is Rob?"

"Rob is very good at what he does," I answered.

"I'm sure he is," she laughed. "We're almost there. I need to slip into my ditzy character."

"Just be yourself." Judy made a rude hand gesture at me.

Professor Ramon met us at the door and led us into the parlor. The other three visitors were already there.

"If you will all excuse me, I need to go and meditate and prepare myself," said Ramon and left the room. I believed he went into the basement to listen in on our conversations in order to garner information to use.

Bart Simmons, Ruth Stone, and Agnes Brompton all seemed eager to start the séance. I couldn't help but feel sorry for them. In their grief and uncertainty they were ripe to be taken advantage of by an unscrupulous asshole like Ramon Decamp. I wasn't sure how I could expose Ramon as a fraud without breaking their hearts in the process.

Judy had slipped into character was talking about Uncle Jack with Ruth Stone. Ruth was happy to share details about her dead son and husband. I noticed that Judy had maneuvered the group over near one of the air registers to make it easier for Ramon to listen in.

In about fifteen minutes Ramon returned and urged us all to sit at the table. "The spirits are strong tonight. I am certain we will have a significant contact tonight. Now if we will all take hands and when I blow out the candle you are not to break the circle."

We did as we were told and when Ramon blew out the candle we were once again plunged into darkness.

"Are there spirits here tonight who want to make their presences known?" intoned Ramon in a very sing-song voice. Suddenly the table lifted up off the ground and seemed to be hovering in the air. I heard Judy gasp in surprise. The others seemed to be taking it in stride. The table suddenly dropped to the floor.

"How many of you are here?" asked Ramon. The table seemed to tilt four times. Ruth Stone grabbed my hand tighter. Suddenly there was a ghostly whisper.

"Judy, Judy," the voice said.

"Judy is here," said Ramon.

"Uncle Jack?" gasped Judy in her cartoon voice. "Is that you?"

"No Judy, it's Sally."

"Sally?"

"Yes, you remember..." but the voice had faded out.

"The weaker spirit has moved on, but I feel another stronger spirit stepping forward." I wasn't sure a spirit without a body could step. But I let it go.

A new "entity" entered the room with a nagging, female voice. "Bart, you better make arrangements soon," said the voice. I confess that if I had to listen to that voice I'd be tempted to hasten her departure for the spirit world. "Bart, I want you to let Professor Ramon advise you. He'll help and you know you can trust him. I'm going now. Heed my words."

59

I couldn't tell where the voice was coming from as it seemed to be everywhere at once, but I knew it wasn't coming from the spirit world.

"Mother, it's me," the voiced sounded like a young male this time.

"Oh, David. I missed you so."

"Thank Professor Ramon, mother. It's his energy that lets me come through."

"Oh, yes David. I will."

"I have something to tell you, mother."

"Tell me dear boy."

"I'm here and..." and suddenly the voice faded.

"Oh, no!" cried Ruth. "He's gone."

Ramon pretended to wake up from his "trance" and reached for the light switch. "There'll be no more messages tonight," he sighed. "The spirits have left us."

"Oh please professor. Could I have a private séance with you?" asked Ruth.

"It's highly irregular," responded Ramon. "But perhaps in your case I could make an exception.

"Oh, thank you professor."

I signaled to Judy that it was time to go. When I looked at her she was as white as a ghost herself. I waited until we got in the car.

"What's the matter?"

"I'm just a little spooked"

"Come on, that was all for show."

"Well, we asked to talk to Uncle Jack."

"And we didn't hear from him did we?"

"No, but we heard from Sally."

"Sally?" I asked. "And who is Sally?"

"Sally was my cousin. She died three years ago."

"That wasn't your cousin Sally. He was taking a shot in the dark. Everyone knows someone named Sally. He was hoping to hit a target. I have a dead aunt named Sally. How do you know it wasn't her?"

"I guess you're right."

"You guess I'm right? Of course I'm right. That tears it. We need to get into that house and prove he's a fake."

"You're going to break into his house? I'm shocked." Judy didn't sound all that shocked at all.

"Of course not," I replied. "I hire that type of work."


"This Professor Ramon Decamp is taking advantage of these poor people and their grief," I was saying to the woman seated across from me.

"We don't like to see that," she replied. "It gives us all a bad name and hurts the victims." Martha Radcliffe was a stout middle-aged woman in a flowing long dress. She was head minister of the Boston Spiritualist Center. I had explained that I was going to expose Ramon Decamp, but that I didn't want to cause the victims more grief. She agreed to help me. "We can explain to them that there are those who wish to take advantage of their losses to make money. We at the center don't charge a fee, and perhaps we can help them reach their loved ones. Do you believe in the afterlife, Mr. Dance?"

"I don't believe or disbelieve, Mrs. Radcliffe. But your sincerity buys a lot of points with me."

"Fair enough, then. If you can set up a meeting with them, I'll try to undo the damage as much as possible."

"Thank you, Mrs. Radcliffe." I got up to go.

"You have an older brother in spirit, don't you? He died when you were about four."

"Yes, I do."

"And your mother is also in spirit?"

"Yes." How in hell did she know that?

"You're a very kind man, Mr. Dance, as much as you try to hide it."

I left and had to admit I was just a bit shaken up.

"I've contacted Ramon's three victims and they've agreed to go with me to the Spiritualist Center next week," offered Judy when we met for lunch at my house. "I didn't tell them the real reason of course."

"I'm glad. I hope they can undo the damage. Now we just need to prove that Ramon is a fake and have him arrested for fraud."

"What do you know about spiritualist churches? Do you think that's any better than what Ramon is doing?"

"I think they are sincere in what they believe. They're not trying to rob anyone, and they offer the believer comfort, so yes I think they will be better off."

"What do you think about them?" asked Judy.

"I am trying to have an open mind. Just before I left Mrs. Radcliffe told me about Julian."

"Julian, your brother? But no one knows about that."

"And that's why I'm keeping an open mind."

# Chapter 9

It was dark when I got up. I hadn't slept well and wasn't looking forward to meeting with the church people even though they were paying me.

"Here, you're going to need a good breakfast to face those pinched faces," said Roscoe as he brought me breakfast. I looked at the tray. He had brought me ham, scrambled eggs, grits, toast, and coffee.

"Grits?"

"I'm a southern boy. And you're going to need some grit for your meeting."

I took a bite. "Actually it's not awful." Roscoe exited the room shaking his head and muttering something about the boss from hell.

I was facing two problems this morning. The most immediate problem was that I needed to get moving on the bishop's murder. I needed to find out why he was in that alley and who, if anyone, he was there to meet. More importantly I needed to make significant progress to justify my fee and expenses.

The second problem I was facing was collecting enough evidence to get Ramon Decamp convicted of fraud and try to mitigate the damage he'd caused to the victims. I had to remember that Ruth Stone's niece was my client, and I needed to report to her, too.

"More Coffee?" asked Roscoe when he came back for the dishes.

"Yes please."

"I see you hated the grits."

I looked at the empty bowl. "Terrible stuff," I replied. "Be sure to buy some more."

"Do you have a final count for the dinner?" Roscoe asked.

"Dinner? I'd almost forgotten about it. It should be around ten or so."

"It's next week, you know."

"So it is, Roscoe. Did you hire some help?"

"I'm interviewing some young men."

"I'll bet you are. Just be sure to give them some breakfast after their 'interview.'"

"They won't be needing any breakfast after I'm done with them."

"I don't even want to know what that means," I said as I dressed to leave.

I presented myself at Bishop Colin Anderson's office promptly at ten. I was led into a small conference room and given a cup of coffee. One wall was dedicated to black and white photos of the previous bishops. The grim, unsmiling faces looking down at me made me feel ill at ease.

"Good morning, Mr. Dance," greeted the bishop as he made an entrance.

"Good morning, your grace," I said as I stood.

"Please call me Colin."

"Only if you call me Jeremy."

"Agreed. Now tell me what you have learned."

"As I've expected, the area where the bishop was found is a place where criminal activity has been happening."

"You think that Bishop Campbell was involved with criminals?"

"He may not have been involved, but his death was certainly a criminal act. He was a member of the Windsor Club, so he may have just been passing through on his way. I intend to find out anything I can."

"Thank you, Jeremy."

"But I'm going to have to find out as much about the bishop as possible. I need you to tell me everything you know about the bishop, no matter how insignificant you think it may be. You can begin by telling what a Midwestern bishop was doing in Boston."

"It takes a lot of money to run a diocese. Angus Campbell was a financial genius. He ran the most prosperous diocese in America. He had a real gift at fund raising." Here the bishop stopped a moment to wipe his eyes. "Sorry, he was also a good friend."

"I understand. Continue when you're ready."

"We were in seminary together. When he retired as a diocesan bishop, I asked him to come here and help out with fund raising. I don't need to tell you how the economy has affected finances. My mission has always been to help the poor, but we barely have enough money to keep the churches open."

"They seem to be doing okay," I observed.

"On Beacon Hill and Back Bay, yes. There are many churches with endowments. You are, I believe, a parishioner at the Church of the Advent."

"Yes, I am." Clearly the bishop had done his own background check.

"There are many other churches outside of Boston that are struggling."

"Who did he work with here in Boston?" I asked, trying to get back on topic.

"He had a group of volunteers. Mostly ladies of the more well-to-do."

"Who did he work with on your staff?"

"Me, of course, but mostly with Tim Black, our diocesan manager."

"Did they get along?" I asked.

The bishop looked shocked. "They were quite fond of each other, I think."

"Did he have any enemies?"

"I can't imagine that he did."

"How about family?"

"He never married. He has a sister and a nephew and I think that's it."

"Any romantic or sexual interests that you know of?"

"He was a man of God!" said the bishop, quite offended.

67

"Men of God are equally human, Colin, and I need to know everything if I'm going to help. You hired me because I'm good at what I do and I'm discrete, so you need to be honest and trust me." I had a feeling that Colin Anderson knew more than he was letting on.

"Very well. I got the impression that Angus wasn't the marrying kind, if you get my drift."

"Yes, I understand. But what makes you think that?"

"Well, there have been incidents."

"Incidents?" This was getting interesting.

"Rumors really. There was speculation that he was involved with the choir director at the cathedral back in the Midwest."

"And?" I asked. It was going to be tough to get a straight answer.

"Well, the choir director was a married man so no one took the rumors seriously."

"I hate to upset your ivory tower view, Colin, but married men often stray with other men. Anyway, what effect did the rumors have?"

"The choir director was fired."

"Who did the firing?"

"The dean of the cathedral."

"So it wasn't the bishop who fired him?"

"No, in fact the bishop was against the firing. Do you think this could be related to the bishop's ..." he hesitated, "...death?"

"Anything is possible. How long ago was this?"

"Over ten years ago, I believe."

"I see. Where was he living while he was here?" I asked.

"The diocese owns some housing units. He was living in an apartment out on Commonwealth Avenue."

"It might be helpful for me to examine his apartment."

"Tim Black is in charge of the business end of the church here in Boston. I'll have him deliver the keys to your home later."

"Thank you for your time, Colin. I'll be in touch in a few days as soon as I learn more."

"Thank you, Jeremy."

I left shaking my head. I didn't know where this investigation was going. My usual cases didn't involve murdered clerics. I was beginning to wonder if I was in over my head.

## Chapter 10

**R**ob and I were sitting in his green Chevy watching Ramon's house. It was dark and cold and Rob had to keep running the car to keep us warm.

"Is this legal?" I asked.

"I'm a police officer and this is an investigation." The porch light went on, the door opened, and Ramon stepped out with a young lady on his arm.

"Bingo," I said. Ramon escorted the young lady to the '28 Ford in his driveway, opened the door for her, and then got in on the driver's side, started up the car, and backed out of the driveway.

"Such good manners," observed Rob.

"I think we should check to see if anyone is at home."

"Good idea, Jeremy. Let's go." We walked up to the house and stepped onto the porch, and rang the bell. We waited.

"Looks like no one is home." I tried the door and the door opened. "He didn't lock his door."

"I think maybe I smell gas," said Rob. "We should be good citizens and check it out."

"Good idea. We'd actually be doing Professor Ramon a favor." Rob pulled a flashlight out of his jacket, and handed it to me. "Do you always carry a flashlight?"

"And a gun," he added.

"Good to know." I led the way into the parlor. I passed the flashlight to Rob and had him hold it while I opened the doors to the armoire. "Well isn't this interesting?"

The armoire was oversized and inside there was a chair and a speaking tube made of some type of fabric covered rubber. At the back of the armoire was what appeared to be a door. After several tries I figured out that it was a pocket door and slid it open. Behind the door was the hall closet.

"It appears that the young lady is able to slip silently into the armoire from the hallway, and exit in the same way," I said. "I'll bet if we look in the parlor we'll find where the speaking tube ends."

"I'm guessing that we'll find it there behind that picture," suggested Rob. On the wall was a framed oil painting on canvas. Rob held the flashlight, and I lifted the painting off the wall. Behind it was a six inch hole lined with tin.

"That explains the voices that seem to float in the air. Let's head into the basement and see if the air vents go anywhere." The door to the basement was under the stairs. I flipped on the lights since it was unlikely to be seen by anyone outside. We went down the stairs. There was a huge coal furnace with heating pipes going every which way, but I discovered two vent pipes that were not connected to the furnace. "You stand here

71

and listen. I'm going up to the parlor and talk. See if you can hear me."

"Okay, good idea," replied rob. I went up the stairs and into the parlor. As soon as my eyes adjusted to the dark I stepped into the parlor. I felt foolish talking to myself, so I recited a few lines from Shakespeare. Shortly after Rob came up the stairs.

"I could hear every word you said. I didn't know you were so fond of *Hamlet*."

"Sure, Shakespeare is my life; now let's get out of here."

"Good idea," agreed Rob. "Let's go."

It was sometime later and Rob and I were sitting in my parlor sipping martinis. Roscoe was in the kitchen throwing something together for dinner. There was a fire burning in the fireplace, and we were both sprawled out in the club chairs before the fire.

"I don't think I want to go out in the cold again," said Rob between sips.

"No need, it's too cozy here."

"It doesn't look like we'll get to sail away in February unless we can solve the bishop's murder."

"It was a nice idea," I replied. "But it doesn't look like we can easily solve it."

"Did you learn anything at your meeting at the diocese?"

"Yes and no." I gave him a summary of the meeting.

"Rumors aren't really a motive for murder, usually. Blackmail, love, money, and revenge are though."

Roscoe came into the room with two trays of food and placed them on the side tables. "I took the liberty of putting fresh sheets on the bed," he said and then winked at us.

"You see what I have to put up with?" I observed as Roscoe smiled and left the room.

"I sure could use someone to look after me," sighed Rob.

"Rob, you have tons of money. I don't know why you live so frugally."

"I'm a cop, so I live like a cop. Most of the time it's fine."

"I think I understand. It frees you from your family."

"That's exactly it. Like you changing your name and moving away."

"Anyway," I said changing the subject. "I'm going to check out Bishop Campbell's apartment if you want to come along."

"Let me take care of a few things at the station tomorrow morning and then I'd be happy to go along."

"It seems like we just broke into a house recently," I said as I slid the key into the lock at Bishop Campbell's apartment.

"We are investigating, not breaking in," Rob reminded me.

We walked into a small hallway that opened up into a large living room. The place was furnished with outdated furniture from the turn of the century. There were heavy drapes at the windows and oriental rugs on the floor. The furnishings were expensive even if they were out of date.

"It looks like the bishop enjoyed the good life,' I said as I looked at the bookcase.

"Who doesn't?"

The bookcase was full of books on theology and some on finance, and strangely enough there were several books devoted to puzzles, which struck me as an interesting combination. I began taking the books down one by one and looking through them.

"What are you doing?" asked Rob.

"People often hide things in books, thinking that no one will think to look there." I picked up the *Book of Common Prayer*, and when I opened it a piece of paper fell out. "See what I mean?"

Rob bent over, picked up the piece of paper, looked at it, and passed it to me. "Nothing but a list of words."

"Maybe we can figure it out later," I said and slipped the paper in my pocket. My search of the rest of the books turned up nothing.

There was nothing unusual in the kitchen or the bedroom. His desk was in order and didn't reveal anything, just an old newspaper with the word jumble half done, and the crossword puzzle completed.

"There's something missing on this desk," said Rob. "Do you see it? Or rather do you not see it?"

I looked at the desk, but couldn't figure out what was missing. "Okay Lieutenant Williams, I give up."

"He doesn't have an appointment book. Anyone who works has an appointment book."

I gave myself a mental slap. "That's true. Everyone needs an appointment book of some type. Maybe he has an office at the diocese."

I picked up the phone and called the cathedral and asked to speak to Bishop Anderson.

"Yes, he has a small office here, and I know that he has an appointment calendar, because I've seen him use it," said Colin Anderson at the other end of the phone line.

"Could you check to see if it's in his office?"

"Of course. I'll call you back. Are you at home?"

"No, but you can leave a message for me with my assistant." I rang off.

"The appointment book might give us some important information," said Rob as we prepared to leave the apartment.

"Maybe," I said. "But as it stands now we don't have much to go on."

"You've had tougher cases," said Rob.

"Yes, but it's only a matter of time before someone leaks the fact that Bishop Campbell's death was no accident."

## Chapter 11

Sometimes mysteries are easily solved, and sometimes important clues jump out at you and lead you to the truth. In both cases I was working on, neither of these things seemed to be happening.

Bishop Anderson called and left a message for me with Roscoe. He had been unable to locate Campbell's appointment book. It was just one more dead end in a case that seemed to have no easy solution.

I was having better luck with exposing Ramon Decamp for my client Donna Jefferson. Her aunt Ruth was indeed the victim of a fraudulent medium. I was all set to expose Ramon; I just had to make sure I didn't do too much damage to his victims. To my mind taking advantage of peoples' grief was the worst type of crime.

I had to put all of these thoughts on hold while I got ready for the dinner party. Roscoe had done most of the leg work, but it was up to me to plan and approve everything. I had to be fitted with a new dinner jacket, decide where the flowers were to be placed, and double check the guest list.

Roscoe had hired temporary help for the evening, and a cleaning service to go through the house before the party.

"How do I look?" asked Roscoe as he tried on his new white chef's smock and hat.

"You look like you belong on a box of cream of wheat," I answered.

"I'm much more handsome than he is."

"That's true," I answered, "but he's not real."

"The hell he's not!"

"And by the way, Amos and Andy are played by two white guys on the radio."

"You are one mean boss. Good thing you pay well," chuckled Roscoe as he left the room.

Roscoe was busy taking a brush to my white dinner jacket as a final touchup for the party. It was still early, and I knew my guests wouldn't be caught dead arriving early, except for Rob Williams and Judy Hogarth, who were given instructions to be here before anyone else.

The guest list was an eclectic mix of people. There was Thomas Atherton, the banker and his wife Barbara. We referred to her as the clueless wonder. She was the only one who didn't suspect that her husband had an eye for the men. Myra Pennington was the social reporter for *The Boston Post*, and rumored to be a lesbian. I had placed her next to Judy at the dining table, hoping they might hit it off. In any case it didn't hurt to have some good publicity.

Aiden Brookfield and Thomas Masson were two confirmed bachelors who together ran a very successful real estate business in Beacon Hill and Back Bay real estate.

Rounding out the list was architect Claus Brandon and his companion Caroline Stanford, and finally Mrs. Bernard Wilmot, as she liked to be called. Mrs. Wilmot was well-known as one of the top art collectors and art patrons in Boston. All the guests had been chosen because they were both successful and interesting. Nothing is worse at a dinner party than boring people.

One of Roscoe's hires was stationed at the door to announce the guests as they arrived, and another one was stationed at the bar to mix the cocktails. Both would help serve dinner later. The third was helping Roscoe in the kitchen.

Roscoe paraded his three hired men in front of me for my approval. They were all immaculately dressed and I gave them the nod. Roscoe was really in his element at a party. He loved the challenge of organizing and preparing for a successful event, and I knew that he took pride in his work.

Rob and Judy arrived together and the three of us retired into my study for a drink before the others arrived.

"This place looks lovely," observed Judy as I steered them upstairs.

"I haven't been to a party for ages," said Rob.

"I don't suppose your policemen friends give many dinner parties," replied Judy.

"Not like this," answered Rob. "But I often get invited to dinner with their families, though.

And they all seem happy enough with what they have."

"Are they still trying to fix you up with eligible young women?" I asked.

"No, I think they've given up on that. Most of them envy my single state."

"Drink up," I instructed. "The others will be here soon."

Myra Pennington was the first to arrive. I knew she would be early so she could observe my guests as they came in. I asked Judy to show Myra around, and the two of them seemed to hit it off.

"Which helper do you think Roscoe going to keep overnight?" whispered Rob.

"Knowing Roscoe, maybe all three," I replied. Rob gave out a low whistle. "Anyway, I hope you're not planning to go home tonight."

"I wouldn't dream of it."

Our conversation was interrupted when Thomas and Barbara Atherton were announced. Barbara is strikingly beautiful, that is until she opens her mouth. After about two minutes in her company you begin to realize that she is dumber than a stump, which worked out well for Thomas.

"Jeremy, it's so good to see you," said Thomas shaking my hand and holding it just a little longer than manners required. "And Rob, I haven't seen you in a dog's age."

"Good to see you, too," returned Rob. "Always a pleasure to see you again Mrs. Atherton."

"Charmed, I'm sure," squeaked Barbara. She must have gotten that line from some movie she saw. "Are you still a copper?"

"Yes, I'm a homicide detective," replied Rob.

"Do your fellow officers know you're the heir to the Williams' fortune?" asked Thomas.

"No they don't, and I prefer to keep it that way."

Aiden Brookfield and Thomas Masson arrived at the same time as Claus Brandon and Caroline Stanford. Myra Pennington made the rounds talking to everyone and I was sure she was gathering information for her next newspaper column. Mrs. Bernard Wilmot was the last to arrive and made quite an entrance.

Sobriety was the first casualty of the evening as the booze was flowing. Mrs. Bernard Wilmot was regaling us all with tales of some of the artists she had known. By the third round of cocktails Roscoe signaled that dinner was ready. My guests more or less staggered to the dining room. Roscoe had done a magnificent job with the place settings. The women were duly impressed, and I noticed Myra had pulled out a little notebook and was taking notes.

The first course was Roscoe's fish chowder. No one in New England can top Roscoe's recipe.

The main course was leg of lamb with mint sauce. Roscoe's helpers were efficient and professional in serving and clearing the table. My guests were effusive with their compliments on the cooking, but they were truly amazed when a dessert of baked alaska was served to them.

"You must have a magician in the kitchen," stated Aiden Brookfield.

"More of a wizard really," I replied. I sent for Roscoe so my guests could praise his skill in person. Roscoe rewarded their compliments with a smile.

Myra Pennington and Judy Hogarth seemed to be hitting it off. They were sitting together in a corner and frequent laughter broke out.

Thomas Atherton was showing signs of being very drunk, and was getting a little too friendly with the other men. His wife Barbara was well beyond sobriety and was chattering away a mile a minute.

We were being served coffee in the parlor when Roscoe hurried in and informed me that a police patrolman was at the door asking for Rob. I signaled to Rob and together we headed to the hall where the patrolman was waiting.

"Sorry to disturb you, lieutenant," said the patrolman. His eyes registered surprise at the sight of Rob in a white dinner jacket.

"What can I do for you O'Brien," asked Rob.

"There's been a murder, sir."

"Couldn't another detective handle it?"

"It's a case you were working on," replied patrolman O'Brien.

"Who was murdered?" I asked.

"Ruth Stone" It was Donna Jefferson's aunt!

"We have the guy who we think did it," relied O'Brien. He took out a small notebook. "It's a Ramon Decamp."

# Chapter 12

It was late morning before I got out of bed. Rob had left earlier to go back to his apartment to shower and change into his work clothes. I was meeting him at the police station later to watch him interview Ramon for the murder of Ruth Stone.

Once I finished breakfast and two cups of coffee I phoned Donna Jefferson to offer my condolences and to arrange a meeting with her.

As soon as I hung up the phone rang again. It was Judy.

"What a wonderful party," she gushed.

"I'm detecting that you had an enjoyable time."

"Oh, yes, very much so."

"So you and Myra hit it off?"

"Oh yes. We're having lunch today. What happened to you last night? You and Rob left and then came back looking very serious."

"Ruth Stone was murdered last night."

"Oh no!" I could tell by her voice that the news upset her. "Why didn't you tell me?"

"I didn't want to ruin the party. Everyone was having a good time, and I knew you were fond of her."

"Was it Ramon who did it?"

"It appears that way. I don't have any of the details yet. I'm meeting Rob at the police station today and hopefully I'll have more information."

"Please call me when you know something," Judy said and then rang off. Roscoe came into my office to clear away the breakfast dishes.

"Which helper did you keep?" I asked him.

"The cute one, of course," he answered back.

"They were all cute."

"So they were," smiled Roscoe as he left the room.

I looked at the clock and figured I had time to clear up some of the accumulated paperwork on my desk.

I gave Roscoe the next two days off as a reward for his hard work. I decided to walk to the police station from Beacon Hill because the weather was mild and the February sun was higher in the sky. The sidewalks were a bit icy and I slid several times as I headed to the Back Bay Police Station.

Rob was at his desk when I arrived. I saw several of his buddies nudge each other as I walked by. They all knew who I was because our paths often cross when I'm on a case. Several of them gave me a nod.

"Good morning lieutenant," I said for the benefit of those listening. Never mind that a few hours ago we were sharing a bed.

"Hello Mr. Dance. Are you ready to watch the interrogation?"

"Let's go." Once we were out of ear shot I added, "Do you think they have a clue?"

"It's not even something they could imagine. So far Ramon has denied having anything to do with her death."

"How did she die?" I asked.

"She was smothered with a pillow. Ramon says that he found her that way when he went to her house for a consultation."

"Who called it in?"

"The niece called the police. She said she saw Ramon holding a pillow over the old lady. When he saw her he ran away."

"It doesn't look good for Ramon, does it?"

"No," said Rob. "It does not."

Outsiders were not usually allowed to sit in on an interrogation, but then again I have friends in high places, and I know where the bodies are buried, so to speak, so it really wasn't an issue. We were in a small windowless room with a metal table and three chairs. Ramon was seated on one side of the table with a very bright light focused on him. He needed a shave, and it looked like he hadn't slept, which I imagine was the case.

"You!" shouted Ramon when he saw me. "What are you doing here? This is a set-up!"

"Sit down Decamp," said Rob. "Unless you want to be put back in handcuffs. Mr. Dance represents Ruth Stone's niece. She hired him because she was afraid you were taking advantage of her aunt."

"I didn't kill anyone," groaned Ramon from his chair as he looked at the floor.

"Here's what we know so far," began Rob. "You've been passing yourself off as a medium and charging exorbitant prices for your services. You have your home rigged with speaking tubes that are used by your accomplice and air shafts through which you can listen to the conversations of your victims. You've been extorting money and preying on the grief of lonely people. And finally you're found holding a pillow over the smothered body of Ruth Stone. Did she discover your fraud and threaten to expose you? Is that why you killed her?"

"I didn't kill her," protested Ramon.

"Then who did?" I asked.

"I don't know; she was dead when I got there."

"You better come clean and tell us your side of the story," stated Rob. "And remember we have a witness."

"Mrs. Stone called me to arrange a private séance."

"You spoke to her then?" I asked.

"She spoke to my..." he hesitated, "assistant."

"So you didn't actually speak to her yourself?"

"No, my assistant takes my messages."

"We've got the police looking for your assistant," said Rob. "It's only a matter of time

87

before we catch her. She'll be charge with assisting the murder."

"She has nothing to do with this," he protested.

"Then it would be helpful if you help us find her, and we can clear all this up," Rob said in a stern voice.

"So you went to the appointment," I said to get us back on track.

"Yes. I knocked and there was no answer. The door was unlocked so I let myself in and called to her. There was no answer. Then I saw her on the sofa with a pillow over her head. I went to her and picked up the pillow to see if she was okay and then the niece came in through the door and started screaming that I killed her, but she was already dead."

"I see," I said after a moment.

"I may be a fraud, but I'm no murderer," sobbed Ramon Decamp as he clung to the table for support.

Rob's team picked up the girl the next day. Her name was Betty Bronson, and she was a farm girl from Vermont, who for some reason found Ramon Decamp attractive. She confirmed that it had been she who took the phone message. She also gave up details about the medium scam that the two of them were working.

"Those old people have all that money. What's wrong with us getting a little bit for ourselves? Beside, Ramon really is a medium and he should get paid for his gift," she had told Rob.

"She doesn't seem to have any idea that Ramon was a fraud," Rob told me later. I found that fact almost as disturbing as the murder.

My meeting with Donna Jefferson was brief. She thanked me for working on the case and proving that Ramon Decamp was a fraud. I presented the bill, and she wrote me a large check.

"It's a sad ending," she said. "But at least it's over."

I wasn't so sure about that.

## Chapter 13

The sun was streaming through the office window when Roscoe appeared with a sandwich for my lunch.

"Want to help me on a case?" I asked.

"Sure thing, boss. Anything to get me out of the kitchen."

"I thought you liked the kitchen."

"I love the kitchen, but a change would be welcome."

"I'm going back to the Windsor Club and check out the back alley tonight, if you want to come along."

"Is it going to be cold?" he asked.

"It's February," I said. "Of course it's going to be cold."

"I'm from Mississippi, you know."

"It's a fact I'm willing to overlook," I sighed. "Are you coming?"

"Of course I am," he laughed as he left the room.

I had just finished my lunch when Roscoe escorted a gentleman into my office. I recognized him as a member of the Windsor Club.

"Mr. Barrymore to see you, sir," announced Roscoe.

"Benjamin, good to see you. What brings you here?" I asked as I got up to shake his hand.

"I need your help," he stated just as Roscoe entered the room with a fresh pot of coffee and a plate of cookies. He stopped when he saw Roscoe.

"Roscoe Jackson is my assistant. You may speak freely in front of him." I nodded to Roscoe and he grabbed a note pad and prepared to take notes.

"I need this to be in complete confidence."

"I understand, Ben. But you know my reputation for discretion."

"Very well. My daughter has run away, and I need you to find her. Can you take the case?"

"As it happens I just finished a case, so yes, I can. Now tell me about your daughter."

"My Marjorie is a head strong seventeen year-old. I fear I've spoiled her."

"As far as I know all seventeen year-old girls are head strong," I replied. "When did she disappear?

"Last Sunday. She went to her boyfriend's house for dinner and never returned."

"Why did she run away?"

"We had a fight."

"I'm going to take a wild guess here and assume it was over a boy?"

"Of course it was over a boy," snapped Ben. I sat back and folded my arms and gave him a cold stare. Roscoe stopped writing and put his pencil down. "Sorry," he apologized. "I'm just worried about her."

"Worry isn't going to find her," I answered. "I need facts. Do you think she ran away with the boy?"

"No, that's just it. The boy is home with his father. He claims he had no idea she ran away."

"I'm going to need names," I said. "I want the name of the boy and the names of all her friends. I want the name of her school, and I want a recent picture of her. You can start by giving Mr. Jackson here the names that you know off the top of her head. Right now you'll have to excuse me while I take care of something."

I went to the kitchen to use the phone. I called the morgue and the local hospitals to see if they had a Jane Doe that had recently turned up. I certainly didn't want her father to hear me calling the morgue, but I wanted to check the obvious before I took the case. No unclaimed females at the morgue and no recent accident victims at the hospitals.

I went back upstairs to my office. "This case is going to take a lot of legwork," I said to Ben Barrymore. "Roscoe, would you give Mr. Barrymore a contract and cost estimate?"

"Yes, sir." Roscoe passed Ben the papers, and I saw the look on his face, but he took the proffered pen and signed.

It was a cold and moonless night. Roscoe parked the car about two blocks from the Windsor Club. Both of us had dressed down for the occasion. Heavy dark pea coats and watch caps helped us blend into the shadows. It also gave us the appearance of dock workers. We walked around the building and into the dark alley.

"I'm getting the feeling," I whispered to Roscoe, "that we are not alone. Let's split up and see if we can get some information."

"I see some movement down this alley," Roscoe whispered back. He headed in that direction, and I headed back out toward the street. I thought I heard footsteps behind me, but when I turned back I didn't see anyone. The alley was a maze that led to other alleys, and I turned the corner and headed toward the back of the Windsor Club. Again I heard footsteps and as I started to turn around I felt a sharp blow on my head and everything went black.

I don't know how long I was out, but when I started to regain consciousness I was back in my bed and an anxious Roscoe Jackson and Rob Williams were standing over my bed. Between them was a man I recognize as my next door neighbor, who was a physician at Mass General Hospital.

"What happened?" I asked, but when I spoke my head began throbbing.

"Someone hit you over the head," answered Roscoe. "I found you passed out in the alley."

"You should have taken me along," said Rob. "You got hurt and didn't find anything out."

"You're wrong," I said, keeping my voice down so my head won't hurt so much. "You look like a cop, and the criminals can smell a cop a mile away. And I did find out something in the alley."

"And what is that?" asked Rob.

"That there is something sinister going on in that alley."

The time passed slowly for the next two days as I was ordered by the doctor to stay in bed. I used the time to update and organize my files. Judy and Rob had practically moved it to look after me and Roscoe kept bringing me hot tea and aspirin and hot soup."

"I need to get out of this bed," I said to Rob when he checked in on me after his shift at the station.

"You need to stay in bed until tomorrow. There's nothing you can do anyway. I'm going to stake out the alley tonight. If I learn anything, I'll let you know."

I tried to get up, but as soon as I moved my head I was stabbed with pain behind my eyes. I fell back on the pillows. "I hate staying in bed."

"You do some of your best work in bed," said Rob with a wicked smile.

"I've got a case you can work on when I'm feeling better," I replied.

The next morning I woke up feeling much better. I made my way to my study where Roscoe served me eggs, bacon, and toast. Judy joined me for coffee when she arrived a few minutes later.

"Any word from Rob?" she asked as she sat down in the red leather chair by the window.

"Not yet," I answered. "It's unlikely he found anything out."

"That's not exactly true," said Rob as he strolled into the room.

"You look like you've been up all night," observed Judy. Rob's clothes were wrinkled, and he needed a shave.

"I have. I went undercover in the alley last night."

"What did you learn?" I asked.

"The alley is a veritable flea market for the underground. I recognized one of the participants as a police informer. He knows the lay of the land, so he's going to ask some questions and report back to me."

"That might be helpful," I added.

"And I see that you're up. You must be feeling better."

"I'm feeling much better thank you. I have a new case to work on that I need to start today. I'll ask Roscoe to run an iron over your clothes, and you can shave and shower before you go back to work. You practically live here; you should leave a suit of clothes here for emergencies."

"Not a bad idea."

It was going to be a busy morning. I had to drop by Ben Barrymore's office and pick up the list of his daughter's friends that he had prepared for me. The list was surprisingly short, and the photo he gave me of her could have been a photo of any teenage girl. The photo wasn't much help as the girl had on the clothe hat which is the current fashion for young ladies. The problem with the hats is that they're pulled down so far that they tend to hide the hair and forehead. Probably not a bad thing in most cases. When I objected Ben went a dug up a photo taken in a studio that was more helpful.

"Why is the list so short?" I asked. "Most young ladies have heaps of friends?"

"She goes to Miss Hampton's School for Young Ladies. It's a small school."

I had heard of the school. It was an exclusive and expensive school. It was also one of those places you know that probably smells like moth balls. I had heard that it was light on the academics and heavy on the domestic arts. Why study algebra and literature when you can study the science of picking up the correct fork at the dinner table?

"Well," I said, "I'll start with the boyfriend and then try the school."

I drove back to the house to pick up Roscoe. I'd need him to take notes while I interviewed the boyfriend and his family. I pulled up in front of the house, honked the horn, and

Roscoe came out the front door carrying his notebook. He was dressed in a gray suit with a gray fedora on his head. The white shirt was a great contrast to his ebony skin. Nobody was going to mistake him for a servant today.

"You're looking pretty sharp, Mr. Jackson."

"Thank you, Mr. Dance. It's a chance to practice my shorthand."

I drove the two of us out to Brookline where the supposed boyfriend of Marjorie Barrymore lived. The house was a small tutor style brick and stucco affair that practically screamed pretentious middle class. The door was answered by the father who introduced himself as Jeffrey Talbot. He was about five nine, heavy set and somewhere between forty-five and fifty. He led us into the living room which seemed to be slightly over burdened with too much furniture.

"I'm Jeremy Dance and this is my assistant Roscoe Jackson. Where looking into the disappearance of Marjorie Barrymore. I understand your son was a friend of hers."

"Yes, please have a seat," he indicated two leather chairs flanking a large radio cabinet. "My son Dan should be home any minute now."

"Could you tell us what you know?" Roscoe pulled out his pencil and notepad.

"My wife died two years ago, and it's just me and Dan. Dan goes to school at Boston Latin and plays sports. I'm not sure how he met Marjorie, but she became a guest here quite often."

"When was the last time you saw her?"

"Last Sunday. Dan had several of his friends from school here for dinner. Marjorie was one of them."

"Did she come with anyone?"

"Yes, she brought a girlfriend with her. I hadn't met her before."

"Where was Dan after the dinner party broke up?'

"Dan was here with me. We listened to the radio until close to midnight."

Just then Dan arrived, and after a short introduction he sat with us and confirmed the information that his father had relayed.

"Apparently," I said, "after she left here she disappeared. Do you have any idea why?"

"No, I don't," Dan answered. "Everyone left at nine. It was a school night, and we broke up early."

"Could you give a list of the guests to Mr. Jackson?"

"Who was the girl she came with? Had you ever met her before?" I had a hunch and I decided to play it.

"Her name was Debbie. I'm not sure if I was told her last name or not. I hadn't ever seen her before."

"Thank you both for your help. I think we have all we need."

"Do you think you can find her?" asked Dan. I could tell that he really cared for the girl.

"I'll try my best."

Back in the car I turned to Roscoe, "I'm going to guess that this Debbie person is not on the list of friends her father gave us."

"Your guess is right, boss."

"If you can find Debbie, I think we'll find Marjorie."

# Chapter 14

**R**oscoe brought my breakfast to me on a tray with the morning newspaper. I was exhausted and had to admit that maybe I wasn't quite fully recovered from my knock on the head. Roscoe had folded the paper in such a way that Myra Pennington's society column caught my eye:

### Beacon Hill Happenings
*By Myra Pennington*

Man about town Jeremy Dance, heir to the Dance Department Stores, was the host of a recent dinner party held in his elegant Beacon Hill townhouse which this reporter was honored to attend. Among the guests were Mr. and Mrs. Thomas Atherton, Mr. Aiden Brookfield and Mr. Thomas Masson, Mr. Claus Brandon and Miss Caroline Stanford, Mr. Robert Williams and Miss Judy Hogarth, and Mrs. Bernard Wilmot.

A pleasant evening of cocktails and conversation was capped off by an elegant candle light dinner. The ladies were dressed in the latest

fashions from New York and
all had a wonderful evening.

I unfolded the paper to read the front page
and immediately realized why Roscoe had
sidetracked me with the society column. The lead
headline screamed: BISHOP'S MURDER
DEEMED SUSPICIOUS. I jumped out of bed and
grabbed the phone.

Bishop Anderson, Archdeacon Peter
Ramsey, and Diocesan Manager Canon Tim Black
were less than thrilled to see me on short notice. I
telephoned and told them to meet me at the
bishop's office.

"Needless to say," I began, "this changes
our plans. If we are going to solve Bishop
Campbell's murder, we have to move quickly, and
I'm going to need your cooperation. So far you've
been holding out on me, giving me as little
information as possible. I don't know what your
game is, but I suspect you are trying to save the
bishop's reputation and keep scandal out of the
church. All worthy goals, I agree, but not very
helpful. The bishop is dead and nothing can hurt
him now, and if the church has anything to hide,
too bad. The church has survived since the time of
Henry VIII, and I don't think whatever it is that
you're hiding will break it now.

"So here's the deal," I said. "Give me the
whole truth, or I can't guarantee that speculation

and cover-ups and criminal activities won't make it to the newspaper."

I was angry, and I was bluffing. I didn't know if they were hiding anything or not, but I knew that if I called their bluff something would happen.

I saw a look pass among them and then Bishop Anderson nodded to the others. "Sit down Mr. Dance. We were hoping you could find the killer without making certain things known."

"Certain things? I told you up front I need as much information as you can give me. Even if you don't think it's at all related."

"I told you up front that Bishop Campbell was a financial wizard," stated Anderson.

"Yes, you did and that he was helping with raising money."

"Well he was also looking into the disappearance of some missing funds."

"How much?"

"About a quarter of a million dollars"

"There's a quarter of a million dollars missing, and you didn't think that it might be related to Campbell's murder?" I was yelling again.

"We didn't want to risk bad publicity. Parishioners would be upset if they knew we mishandled money."

"Well now, thanks to your inability to trust me, we have a public who now thinks that Bishop Campbell's death was most likely murder." I banged my fist on the table for emphasis. "I want some answers!"

I left the bishop's office and headed home. I needed time to think and sort out the mess that these dunderheads had caused. I guess I was being too hard on them. Criminal activity wasn't something they were used to dealing with. Missing funds and murder were commonplace for some of us, but probably the clergy didn't know what to do. I decided to let them stew for a while until I could come up with a new plan.

"Woman here to see you, Mr. Jeremy," said Roscoe as he met me at the door.

"Send her away Roscoe. I've had enough for one day."

"I think you'll want to see this one." Roscoe had said "woman to see you," and not "lady to see you." It was a code. Lady meant money, and woman didn't."

"Where is she?"

"In the parlor."

"Send her up to my study," I sighed.

"I'll bring some tea, too."

"Thank you."

I sat at my desk and tried to look business-like when she entered. She was about twenty-five, blonde in a way that made me think of peroxide, and quite petite.

"Come in Miss Bronson," I said.

"How did you know? I didn't tell your butler my name."

"You fit the police description. And Mr. Jackson is my assistant, not my butler. Now what can I do for you? No wait, let me guess. You've come here to see if I can help clear your boyfriend Ramon from the murder charge?"

Betty Bronson looked at me as if I had just pulled a rabbit out of my hat while sawing a woman in two. Then she started to cry. Roscoe entered with the tea tray, quickly took in the situation, and produced a handkerchief for Miss Bronson. I signaled Roscoe to grab his notebook and sit down.

"When you're ready Betty, tell me what you'd like me to do," I said more gently.

"Oh, Mr. Dance," she sobbed. "Ramon couldn't kill anyone. You've got to help us. I want you to prove that Ramon is innocent." She reached into her handbag and took out a twenty dollar bill and placed it on the desk. I could tell by looking at her that twenty-dollars for her was a small fortune.

"Betty, all the evidence points to Ramon as the killer. I don't think there's anything I can do. And I'm not convinced that he didn't kill Ruth Stone."

"Please Mr. Dance, you're my only hope. Please just go and talk to Ramon. I've got a job now and I can pay you."

I passed Betty back her twenty dollars. "I'll go see him, and if I believe he's innocent, I'll help you. But if he's guilty anything I find out I'm turning over to the police. Do you have a dollar bill Miss Bronson?"

"Yes."

"Then give it to Mr. Jackson for a retainer. He'll write you a receipt. Come back the day after tomorrow and I'll tell you if I'll take the case or not."

"Oh, thank you Mr. Dance."

"Roscoe," I said after she had left, "I think I need a cocktail."


Dance music filtered out through the door of the Starlight Club as the four of us entered for a late supper. We were seated far from the band to make conversation easier. Myra and Judy, Rob and I had decided to have an evening out. To the public eye it appeared that we were two couples out on a double date, of course they had no idea that the two couples were boy-boy and girl-girl.

"I'm working on three cases right now, and I'm going to have to hire some outside help," I explained to Judy and Rob when Myra excused herself to greet some old friends. I thought it best not to mention my business in front of a reporter.

"Do you really think Ramon Decamp is innocent?" asked Judy.

"He's a snake, but that doesn't make him a murderer."

"As far as the police are concerned, he's the guy," said Rob.

"And he most likely is, but I promised his girlfriend I'd look into it. I know you have your hands full now that the bishop's death has made the papers."

"We're under a lot of pressure by the public. So far they are satisfied that the police are investigating, but we need to have some answers soon," sighed Rob.

"What are you all talking about?" asked Myra when she returned to the table.

"I was just saying," I replied, "that I feel like dancing." I took her hand and led her to the dance floor.

# Chapter 15

Johnny Merrill was sitting in the red chair in my office as I handed him a list of Marjorie Barrymore's friends and classmates. Johnny was a private investigator I used from time to time. He was much better at legwork than I, and he had the ability to blend into a crowd, which I lacked. He was somewhere in the neighborhood of forty, average size and looks.

"If we can find the mysterious Debbie, we will probably get a line on the missing girl. The father is rich, so expenses won't be an issue. Just make sure you keep good records," I said as I handed him a hundred dollars.

"Don't worry; this isn't the toughest case you've given me."

"Good. Give me a progress report tomorrow morning. If I'm not here, you can give the details to Roscoe." I walked him to the door.

As soon as I finished my cup of coffee, I grabbed my coat and headed off to Charles Street Jail to visit Ramon Decamp. It was a short walk down Bowdoin Street, past Massachusetts General Hospital, to the Charles Street Jail.

I was seated in a small interview room when Ramon was brought into to me. He was handcuffed and looking as he had been roughed up a bit.

"Your girlfriend, Betty Bronson, has hired me to try and prove that you didn't kill the old lady. Frankly, I'm not convinced that you're innocent, but I always try to help my clients."

"I thought you worked for the niece?"

"I did and we've completed our arrangement. Now I need you to tell me exactly what happened."

"But you've already heard the story."

"Tell me again. I'm trying to help you."

"Ruth Stone called me to arrange a private consultation."

"Did you speak to her?"

"No, Betty answered the phone and made the appointment." At least this backed up what Betty had told me.

"So you didn't speak to her yourself?"

"No."

"What happened when you went to her house?"

"I rang the bell. There was no answer. I tried the door and it was unlocked. I called out to her, but there was no answer. When I went into the living room, I saw her on the sofa. She had a pillow over her face. I rushed over and removed the pillow just as the niece arrived. She started screaming when she saw me and went out the door yelling 'murder!'"

"Then what?"

"I grabbed her arm and felt for a pulse, but there was no pulse, and she was cold."

"She was cold? What do you mean she was cold?"

"Her hand was ice cold."

"If her hand was cold then she was dead for a while. Did you tell the police this?"

"I don't remember. It was all such a nightmare." I made a mental note to ask Rob to check the police report.

Lyle Compton invited me to lunch at the Windsor Club. I had no illusions that this was a social call. Now that the public knew that Bishop Campbell's death might not have been an accident, I knew he was worried that the club might be linked to the death.

"As you know," he said as I studied the lunch menu, "anonymity one of the major reasons gentlemen join this club." I could have pointed out some more obvious reasons, but I decided to listen. "We keep a low profile here. Most people don't even know we exist."

The waiter came over and took our orders. "I always enjoy the chicken aspic here," I replied just to make him squirm a bit.

"What I mean to say is," he continued, "this unpleasantness could bring us some publicity, and we want to avoid that."

"Lyle, you didn't invite me here to tell me things I already know, did you?"

"No, it's just that we found something that was left here the night the bishop was here, and we don't know what to do with it."

"You could give it to the police," I said.

"Well, it's just that we want to avoid the police if possible. They may wonder why we haven't turned it over to them before now."

"Why didn't you?"

"We only just found it yesterday when the janitor was cleaning up one of the bathrooms. It was hidden behind the toilet tank."

"What was hidden?" I asked. I had no idea where this was going. He reached into his jacket and pulled out a four by six inch envelope and put it in front of me.

"This is what he found."

I opened the envelope, pulled out the article, and let out a low whistle. It was Bishop Campbell's missing appointment book!

It was getting late and I was hungry. I had spent two hours studying the appointment book and still didn't have a clue as to what I was looking for. Rob Williams sat across from me and tried his hand at interpretation as I read aloud the entries.

"Are you seeing any pattern in his appointments at all?" he asked.

"There are several entries that seem to have regular appointments. Every Monday at six there is a meeting with SM."

"Just initials?"

"Yes. Other entries he either uses phrase that make no sense like 'Smears I Try.'" Just then Roscoe entered with two dinner trays.

110

"You must be a mind reader," I said as he sat the trays down.

"Don't need to read your mind. I've worked with you long enough to know when to feed you."

"Thanks Roscoe, you are worth your weight in gold."

"Anything else I can do for you?"

"Lieutenant Williams, in his official capacity, will need to take this appointment book to the police station tomorrow for possible evidence. Before it leaves this house, I'd like you to copy the relevant information from it."

"Will do, boss," he said as he left the room.

"The most important entries are most likely the ones on the day he was killed," said Rob.

"The problem with that is that the entry for the evening just said 'dinner' and 'lamb tick.'"

"I assume that 'dinner' means dinner at the Windsor Club, but what the hell does 'lamb tick' mean?"

"No idea and it's making my head hurt," I complained.

"I might have a cure for that," said Rob with a look I knew quite well.

"I bet you do," I answered.

We were having breakfast in the kitchen and Roscoe was hovering over us making sure our coffee was hot.

"Sit down, Roscoe. We're capable of pouring our own coffee,' I growled.

"Someone have a rough night?" Roscoe asked Rob as he took a seat and poured himself a cup of coffee.

"Talks in his sleep," muttered Rob. Neither of us was any good before the caffeine kicks in.

"Don't forget to copy out the appointment book," I reminded Roscoe.

"Already done it," he said and he handed the book to Rob.

"So what are you going to do today?" asked Rob.

"I'm juggling three cases," I sighed. "I need to do some leg work on the Ramon Decamp case, and then I have to meet with Johnny Merrill to see if he made any progress in the missing girl case."

"You're wasting your time with Ramon. It's an open and shut case."

"Maybe," I said. "And maybe not."

# Chapter 16

**R**uth Stone's house was out on Commonwealth Avenue, and I thought it would be a good idea just to check out the area. I hopped a trolley at Park Street and headed out toward Kenmore Square. There was about an inch of slush on the ground because the weather kept alternating from warm to cold in typical February fashion.

It was the middle of the morning, and the street was deserted with only an occasional automobile passing by. Her house was one in a series of townhouses arranged on both side of the street. I located her house, and then looked around at the neighboring houses. As I looked at the house directly across the street I saw movement behind the lace curtain in the bay window. I knew exactly what that meant.

Every neighborhood has at least one elderly lady who spends her time watching the street and the neighborhood, and usually has a good idea of what's going on. I walked over to the house and rang the doorbell.

The woman who answered was in her seventies, was dressed in black, and had her white hair tied up in a tight bun.

"I'm sorry to bother you," I said as I handed her my card, "but I recently worked for Ruth Stone and was hoping you could help me."

"Pleased to meet you," she looked at the card, "Mr. Dance. I'm Agnes Parker. Such a terrible thing. Imagine murder here on the avenue."

"I'm looking into her death and was hoping maybe you could help me."

"Come in Mr. Dance and have a seat. Would you like some tea?"

"Yes, thank you Mrs. Parker." I was pretty sure I hit the jackpot for neighborhood gossip. She returned with a tea tray with some very good looking cookies on it.

"Are you the Mr. Dance I read about in the society columns?"

"Guilty, I'm afraid."

"Oh, this is exciting."

"If I could ask you some questions, it would be most helpful."

"I'll help if I can," she smiled.

"On the day that Mrs. Stone was murdered, did you notice anything unusual?"

"Well of course I don't spy on my neighbors," she said. "But I just happened to be washing my windows that day and might have seen something."

"Did you see a man enter the house?"

"Yes, I did. The paper said it was Mr. Decamp."

"Could you describe him?" I asked. "Just to make sure it was the same man." She gave a fairly detailed description of him.

114

"What did he do when he went to the house?"

"He knocked on the door, called out something I couldn't hear, and then tried the door. It was open and he walked in. A few minutes later the niece came out screaming. I tell you it was most upsetting."

"How long was it between the time that the niece entered the house, and the time that she came running out?"

"I don't understand?" she said.

I repeated the question.

"But she never entered the house. She was already there."


Okay, so maybe Ramon Decamp was telling the truth, or maybe he wasn't. At least in my mind I had enough questions to keep moving on the investigation. But it wasn't my only case, and I felt that right now time was more critical in finding Marjorie Barrymore.

Johnny Merrill was ushered into my office by Roscoe. His disheveled appearance, I hoped, was part of his undercover operation.

"I interviewed all her friends," he said without the preamble of a greeting.

"And what did you learn?"

"None of them has a clue who this Debbie is. She suddenly started to hang out with the Barrymore girl about a week before she disappeared. One of her friends thought the girl's last name is Rankin, or something like that."

"Not the most helpful information we have is it?"

"I went through the phone book and called all the Rankins in the area. No one admitted to knowing a Debbie."

"We seem to be at a dead end," I sighed.

"Not exactly," replied Johnny as he reached into his pocket and pulled out a photo. "This was taken at the boyfriend's party. It shows the two girls in the foreground."

I looked at the photo. Both girls looked amazingly alike in both dress and facial features, but then I imagined that most teenage girls do. I wasn't the best judge of women's fashion, but they both looked well-dressed.

"Good work Johnny. Go have some copies made and we can begin to circulate the images and see if we get a hit."

"Will do," he said as he got up to leave. "What about expenses?"

"Do whatever you need; daddy's got deep pockets, but just keep an account."

It was Roscoe's night off, and I gave him the car. I was dining at the Windsor Club with Rob. We had a table off in one corner away from the ears of my fellow club members. I was telling him of my recent visit to Ruth Stone's neighborhood.

"According to the nosey neighbor, the niece, Donna Jefferson, was already in the house when Decamp discovered the body."

"Do you think she's reliable?"

"Old ladies with not enough to do often know lots of things. But of course it's not evidence."

"It also doesn't mean anything. Maybe she went in the house the back way, and even if she lied about entering the house, he still most likely killed her. I imagine the shock of what Donna Jefferson saw most likely affected her memory," Rob said as he sipped from his glass of wine.

"Well, I have an idea I want to pursue," I added.

"What is that?"

"I'll let you know if anything pans out."

"How's the case of the missing girl?"

"I think I've reached a dead end. The father doesn't want the police involved, and I'm not too sure they would have any better luck."

"It's not a kidnapping?"

"No, there's been no ransom demand."

"And she didn't run away with the boyfriend?"

"No and I think he doesn't know anything at all."

"No clues?"

"All I have is this photo to go on." I passed it to Rob. "It's a picture of the girl and her mysterious friend Debbie at the party where they were last seen."

"Which one is which? They both look alike."

"That's the problem. One teenage girl looks pretty much like another. Now it's my turn," I said. "Have the police any new clues on the bishop's murder that I should know about?"

"I'm meeting my informant later tonight. He's been working the alley for a few days. You want to come along?"

"You know I do."

"To us," he said as he held up his wine glass.

"To us," I responded as we clinked glasses.

# Chapter 17

The evening was cold and raw and freezing rain was showering the city in an icy embrace. Rob and I left the Windsor Club and tried our best not to fall on the slippery sidewalk. It was only three blocks to the bar where we were to meet Rob's informant, but it took us twice as long to get there as we frequently slipped and fell. Okay, so I slipped more times than Rob. It was probably because I was two months older.

"That's him at the bar," said Rob as he pointed to a small older man in a tattered suit. We went over to the bar and we took our seats on each side of him.

"You got anything for us O'Malley?" asked Rob without preamble.

"Who's this?" he asked and inclined his head in my direction.

"My buddy. You can trust him."

"If you say so, Williams."

"What's the word, O'Malley?"

"I checked. It was New Year's Day evening. Not a good selling day. None of the usual vendors wasted their time in the alley. Of course I don't know about the usual whores. They don't keep regular hours."

"You know the whores?" I asked.

"Yup."

"Any of them dangerous?" asked Rob.

"Nope."

"Anything else?" I added.

"Nope."

I handed him ten dollars. He took it, put it in his pocket, and then walked out of the bar.

"I just thought of something," I said. "I'm so stupid I should have thought of it before."

"What?"

"We tried to create a story to explain the reason the bishop was in alley. We said maybe that he was going to Gibby's. So, what if he really *was* going to Gibby's? Did you guys check that out?"

"No, it was just something we made up." I watched Rob's face as the truth dawned on him. "Let's go."

"Where?"

"Gibby's of course."

Gibby's was an upscale establishment that had made it through the worst of the depression without missing a beat. The interior was dark wood and small tables set with white tablecloths and shining silverware. Candlelight was in abundance and there was always the tinkling of glasses. The whole atmosphere was one of intimacy and elegance. Jacques, the maitre d' recognized me as we entered.

"Good evening Mr. Dance. Would you like a table for two?"

"Good evening, Jacques. This is Police Lieutenant Robert Williams. We were hoping you

120

could give us some information." Rob slipped him a ten dollar bill as they shook hands.

"Of course Mr. Dance, what can I do for you?"

"Would you be so kind as to check your reservations for January first and tell me if there was a reservation for Bishop Campbell?" Jacques pulled out a notebook from under his stand and flipped through the pages.

"There was a reservation for a table for two for an Angus Campbell."

"Did he keep the reservation?" asked Rob.

"No, he didn't show up. We finally had to give the table away."

"Thank you," I said.

"I'll bet if we knew the identity of the dinner guest, we would know the identity of the killer," remarked Rob as we left the restaurant and began looking for a taxi.

Roscoe had a roaring fire going in the parlor when we returned to Beacon Hill. We were cold and wet and Roscoe served us brandy as we settled by the fire.

"No sense of going back out into the nasty night," I said to Rob.

"No there isn't; though I'm not spending much time at my apartment lately, and I seem to be relying on your hospitality too much this winter."

"Not at all, and you know better."

"Just thought I'd check."

Roscoe came back into the room. "Miss Judy called this evening and invited you to lunch tomorrow. She said to meet her at noon for chop suey at the Golden Dragon on Charles Street."

"Do I need to call her?"

"Only if you can't make it." Just as I finished there was a loud crash of pots and pans that seemed to come from the kitchen. Roscoe just rolled his eyes.

"I take it you are not alone in the kitchen?"

"Not tonight," he said and laughed.

Rob had left for work in the early morning and after I paid some bills and wrote a long letter to my sister it was time to head out to Charles Street for lunch with Judy. It took me some time to locate The Golden Dragon. It was in a basement of an area I frequently walked by, but I had never noticed it before.

The restaurant was filled with doctors and nurses from Mass General around the corner and seemed to be quite popular. Judy was sitting over in the corner cradling a cup of tea as if she was trying to warm her hands. She was dressed in a smart pink suit with a matching hat. She must have sensed my approach because she looked up as I headed across the room to her table.

"There you are," she said. "I thought you were lost."

"Sorry to be late." I replied as I sat down. "I guess I never noticed this place before. It seems to be quite popular."

"The chop suey is very good and the prices are very cheap." She poured me a cup of tea from the steaming Chinese tea pot. An Asian waiter in a white jacket came to our table and placed the menus before us. Judy held up two fingers and the waiter scooped up the menus and hurried away.

"Did you just order?" I asked.

"Yes, I'm paying so I ordered. Besides you know nothing about Chinese food."

"That's true," I admitted. "So what's on your mind? It's not more woman trouble is it?"

"Not at all. Myra and I really hit it off."

Just them the waiter arrived bearing two steaming dishes of food I couldn't identify. I tentatively stuck my fork into the food and tasted it. It was very good.

"What's in it?" I asked.

"From what I understand, it's a little bit of everything. Surprisingly good isn't it?"

"Yes, indeed. So I know you're bursting to tell me something. What is it?"

"Well, you're working for that horrible Ramon Decamp right?

"I'm working for the girlfriend actually. I don't think the poor thing is all there."

"Do you think Ramon killed Ruth Stone?"

"I have my doubts."

"Why?" asked Judy as she dug into her chop suey.

"I have a witness that says the niece was already in the house. And Ramon says that the body was cold when he touched it."

"He could be lying."

"Of course he could be. Why are you interested all of a sudden?"

"It turns out that Myra is a good friend of the niece."

"And you learned something didn't you?"

"The niece has no money of her own. She lived off her aunt's charity. But Myra gave the impression that the old lady wasn't all that fond of her and only supported her out of a sense of duty."

"This is interesting," I said as I finished the chop suey on my plate. "Do you think Myra is up to a little investigating?"

"I'm sure she'd love to do it. You know how she loves to wheedle information out of people. It's what makes her a good reporter."

"She writes a society column," I reminded her.

"Still I'll bet she can help."

"Okay then," and I outlined what I wanted Myra to find out for me.

Rob had called earlier and was working on a case which meant that I wouldn't see him for a few days. I always wondered what his other life was like. He kept pretty true to the cop image, living as he does on just a cop's salary. He had tons and tons of money, but as far as I could see he only spent it when he was with me.

"Got any plans tonight, Roscoe?" I asked as he passed by my study.

"No, what do you need?"

"Some company. I don't feel like being by myself. How about we take a walk, find a bar, and have a few drinks?"

"Are you buying?"

"Of course."

"Then I'm drinking."

It was a still night and not too cold and we walked into the center of the city, past Dance's Department Store.

"How come you never shop there, seeing that your family owns it?"

"It's my grandparents who own it, and I don't want the employees to fall all over themselves when they know I'm the grandson of the founder."

"You are a strange one, Boss."

"Thanks." We walked along the street and turned down toward city hall and I spotted a bar called The Tabard. "Let's try in here."

We walked into the bar and there was the usual clinking of glasses and the loudness of chatter. Suddenly the chatter died down as everyone began looking at us. The bartender looked up. Put down the glass he was filling with beer, and came toward us as we stepped further into the bar.

"We don't allow no pansies and no nigg..." The bar tender never finished his sentence, mostly because my right fist hit him in the mouth before he could say anything rude. Plus my left fist made contact with his stomach, and as he double over, my knee accidently made contact with his jaw on his way down toward the floor.

Roscoe grabbed my arms and pulled me out of the bar and out into the street.

"Let's get out of here, Boss"

"I'm almost positive that my grandparents own this block of buildings," I said as I tried to get my breath back. "A couple of phone calls, and I think The Tabard will be surprised to learn that their lease has just expired.

"You are one mean son-of-a-bitch," said Roscoe, and I thought I heard a hint of admiration in his voice.

# Chapter 18

The sun was shining through the windows of my study as I set about to begin my day. Roscoe had just brought me a breakfast of dropped eggs on toast when Rob called.

"Did you stay up all night on a case?" I asked.

"Almost all night. I did get to go home for about three hours of sleep. I was wondering if you knew anything about a disturbance at a bar last night?"

"Why would you think I had anything to do with a bar brawl?"

"Let's see, I've known you since freshman year at Andover. You have a hair trigger temper when it comes to social issues, and the description of the two men was pretty close to that of you and Roscoe."

"This is Boston and there must be thousands of men fitting our description."

"There are indeed. I just thought it was interesting that the bar was in a building owned by your grandparents."

"Oh my," I said in mock horror. "It does look bad for me. I congratulate you on your detective abilities."

"You want to tell me what really happened?"

I told him.

"I don't blame you then. I suppose the bar will be evicted?"

"No doubt. How do you know all this anyway? I didn't think homicide concerned itself with bar brawls."

"There was a shooting in the bar around midnight, so we had to ask about any unusual events during the evening. Well, here's the interesting part. The victim's name was Bill Rogers, and he was a janitor at the Episcopal diocese offices. He was having a drink at the bar, and a guy walked up to him and shot him."

"Did anyone see the shooter?"

"Everyone saw the shooter, but no one can describe him other than to say he was ordinary looking and wore loose clothing. The place erupted in panic, so no one got a good look at him."

"You think it might be related to the bishop's murder?"

"Maybe or maybe not. It's worth looking into, however."

"Well, let me know what you find out."

"I'll stop by tonight if that's okay."

"Sure thing. It might cost you though."

"It always does," he laughed and hung up.

Rob and I were having a late night supper by the fire in the parlor while we were reviewing my three cases. I needed a break pretty soon because, if the truth were told, I was stuck.

"According to Ramon Decamp," I said, "Ruth Stone's body was already cold when he felt for a pulse."

"That's interesting. I'll check the coroner's report for the time of death. But he could have killed her earlier."

"Then why did the niece say that he had the pillow in his hands as if he was caught in the act of suffocating her?"

"You think the niece is lying?"

"It's a possibility," I answered.

"What about the missing girl?" asked Rob, switching the conversation to my other case.

"Johnny Merrill interviewed all her friends, but all he came up with was the photo, and it doesn't seem to be much help. I've reached a dead end on this case."

"You'll think of something," said Rob. "You always do."

"At least with the bishop's murder, we know that he had a dinner engagement and that he was on his way to Gibby's. If we can find out who he was meeting, we might have a lead on the killer."

"The police have his appointment book. But it's mostly gibberish as far as we can tell."

"I keep looking at the copy Roscoe made, but I can't make heads or tails out of it at all."

"Maybe we should just go to bed and forget about it," suggested Rob.

"That," I said, "is the best offer I've had all day."

The shooting of the janitor who worked in the same office building as Bishop Campbell added another dimension to the case. I'm not sure there was a connection, but it was something that I needed to explore. I knew that the police would be there asking questions, so I waited until the afternoon to head over to the diocese offices.

Bishop Colin Anderson looked tired and forlorn as I entered his office.

"Allow me to express my condolences on the death of one of your staff members," I said.

"Thank you, Jeremy," he said with a weak smile.

"I'm sure the police have already asked you all the questions, but would you mind answering them for me?"

"If it will help," he sighed. "Have a seat, Jeremy."

"What was the relationship between the bishop and the janitor?"

"The janitor worked in the building, but he had very little contact with the staff unless he met them while he was doing his rounds."

"What were his usual duties?"

"He would come in early and make sure the coal furnace was stoked up. He washed the floors once a week or more often if it was mud season. He emptied out the wastebaskets, put out the garbage, and did minor repairs around the building."

"Who on the staff did he take his orders from?"

"Tim Black was in charge of the building and grounds, along with his financial duties."

"Do you know any reason why someone would kill him?"

"I'm afraid I don't."

"Thank you for your time, Bishop Anderson," I said as we shook hands.

I walked down the hall and stood in the doorway of Tim Black's office. He was on the phone, but he looked up and waved me in.

"I suppose you're here about the shooting death of Bill Rogers," Canon Black said when he hung up the phone.

"I'm trying to see if there is a connection with the bishop's death."

"I understand," he said.

"Do you have any idea why someone would want to shoot your janitor?"

"Bill Rogers was a gambler. I'm wondering if he owed money to the wrong people."

"How do you know he was a gambler?"

"He's asked to borrow money from me on several occasions."

"Large amounts?"

"Not really. Ten dollars here and ten dollars there."

"I see," I said. "Any other thoughts?"

131

"I've been racking my brain all day, but that's all I have."

"Thanks for your time."

"Any new developments on Bishop Campbell's murder?"

"I'm exploring a few new leads," I said. "I'll let you know how they pan out. Did you tell the police about his gambling problem?"

"No, I wasn't sure they needed to know. We don't need any more bad publicity."

"What can you tell me about the man?"

"Bill Rogers was an outgoing, friendly man who had lots of friends."

"How do you know that?"

"He always seemed to have visitors stopping by to see him on breaks and lunches."

"What type of visitors?"

"Mostly men, but a few women here and there."

"Any family?"

"None that he mentioned."

"Could I see his personnel file?"

"I guess so," he said as he went to a large file cabinet in the corner, fished around in the drawers, and pulled out a file. "Are you investigating his death, too?"

"Only in as far as it may or may not relate to Bishop Campbell's murder." I took the folder and read through it. No family except a sister in Worchester. His address was a rooming house out in Dorchester. I jotted down a few notes, but was pretty sure I wouldn't need them.

The sun was higher in the sky and the temperature was above freezing, which in February is a good thing. I walked up to Park Street and took the subway, and got off at Bowdoin Street and walked up Beacon Hill.

Roscoe was going through my closet gathering clothes for the dry cleaner and the laundry service. Roscoe always checks my pockets because I have a habit of putting things in my pockets and forgetting them.

"This paper here had Bishop Campbell's name on it," he said as he passed me the paper. "Thanks Roscoe, It's the paper I found in the bishop's prayer book. I had picked it up, placed it in my pockct, and promptly forgotten about it."

"Looks like just a list of words to me."

"That's the puzzle. Why was it in his prayer book?"

"The old man was probably forgetful. Most old people are."

"It's not just old people who are forgetful apparently," I observed.

## Chapter 19

It was early evening and music was playing on the radio as Rob and I enjoyed our second pre-dinner cocktail. Rob had a rare day off, and we had spent it taking a drive out into the country for lunch. We had found a seafood place on the south shore and had a lunch of seafood chowder, fried clams, and chocolate cake. We were both a little tired from the drive, so I gave a groan when the doorbell rang.

"I hope it's not a case," I said. "I have three already and not doing very well on any of them."

"Maybe it will be an easy one for you."

The parlor door flew open and my sister Velda walked in. I was on my feet and across the room in seconds to give her a big hug.

"Velda, what are you doing here? I thought you were in Berlin?"

Velda is my twin sister. She is just about thirty minutes older than I am, and she rarely lets me forget that she is my big sister.

"Berlin is not such a nice place with Hitler's Nazi party taking over. They're setting up for the Olympic Games and there are all types of activity going on. All of Europe is getting to be a bore. I can paint anywhere."

"When did you arrive?"

"The ship sailed into New York harbor this morning, and I got on the train and came here to see you. I've had the most awful Atlantic crossing."

"You remember Rob?" I asked. Rob got up to give her a hug.

"How are you Sergeant Williams?"

"It's Lieutenant Williams now."

"Well lieutenant, you are still the handsomest man in the world."

"And you're still the prettiest woman in the world."

"But not," she gave a mock sigh, "as pretty as my brother."

Roscoe came into the room. "I've made up the guest room and placed Miss Velda's bags upstairs."

"Thanks, Roscoe," he smiled and left the room. "I'm surprised you didn't head to Philadelphia to see dad and step-mom."

"To hell with them," said Velda. "When they sent you away that was the last straw. They only care about their money and their position."

"They didn't send me away so much as I took the excuse to get away," I admitted.

"And that's to your credit. We have our own money, so we only need to send them a letter now and then."

"How long are you staying?" asked Rob.

"I thought I sponge off you guys for a few weeks and then head to the Maine coast and set up a studio when the weather warms up."

"You stay as long as you like," I offered. "Are you hungry?"

"Starved!"

"I'm sure Roscoe is in the kitchen fixing something fancy to celebrate."

"Well for god's sake get me a drink!" she said as she sat on the sofa and took off her shoes.

We had dinner in the dining room. I was pleased to see that my sister could still pack away the food.

"So are you living here now, Rob?" my sister asked after the soup was served.

"It seems more and more that I am," he admitted.

"Rob likes to live simply when he's playing cop," I said.

"Silly really," my sister said bluntly. "You've all the money in the world."

"I want to feel useful. I want some structure to my life."

"And then we have my brother playing at being a detective."

"He's very good you know," answered Rob defending me.

"I guess I understand. I have my painting. If I didn't have it I end up being one of those pieces of society fluff you read about in the papers."

Roscoe appeared with a platter of fried chicken, and we all dug in.

"At least," Velda said as she looked at us, "You have each other."

I had to agree.

Later my sister put in a long distance call to our dad. He sounded relieved that she was back in the states. She passed the phone to me, and I spoke with him briefly and told him that things were fine. "And Rob sends his regards," I said and hung up.

Miss Hampton's School for Young Ladies was located at the end of a trolley line in the more fashionable town of Brookline. Velda insisted on coming with me to interview the head mistress and teachers of Marjorie Barrymore. Velda is always afraid that I might miss something, and she believes that her female intuition is more accurate than my fact gathering.

The school was in a rather large three-story wood framed building with ugly-looking fire escapes on both sides of the structure.

"Looks like a mill workers' boarding house," observed Velda as we stepped out of the Cadillac.

"Or a reform school."

We walked up the sidewalk, knocked on the door, and were led into a small reception room by a rather dour looking elderly woman dressed in black.

"Miss Hampton will be with you directly," the woman said and then slipped out of the room.

"Where's the funeral?" asked Velda.

"Are you going to behave yourself?" I asked her.

"We'll see."

Miss Hampton came in and introduced herself. She was about sixty years old, rather plump, and was wearing a long black dress with lavender panels. She had a pair of reading glasses attached with a black ribbon handing around her neck.

"I'm looking into the disappearance of Marjorie Barrymore; I was hoping you could give me some background information."

"I'll do my best," she said. "We are all very concerned about her."

"What type of student is she?" I avoided using the past tense when speaking of her.

"She's very bright in her academic courses, but only average in the domestic sciences."

"Domestic sciences?" asked Velda.

"You know, cooking, sewing, painting, and running a household. Skills they'll need when they are married."

"Yes, I see," I said before Velda could respond. I glanced over and my sister had turned pale. I gave her a warning look to keep quiet. Velda had some definite ideas on marriage that I'm sure wouldn't have been of interest to Miss Hampton.

"Did she get along with the girls here?"

"Actually she was quite popular, but she was more of a follower than a leader."

"Was there any change in behavior prior to her disappearance?"

"Now that you mention it, she had seemed much more subdued during the week before she disappeared."

"Do you have any ideas on why she would have disappeared?" I asked.

"No, none at all."

"Thank you Miss Hampton," I said as we got up to leave. "You've been most helpful?'

"Have I?"

"Yes," I said. "You have."

Back in the car Velda looked at me with a puzzled look. "Exactly what did you learn that was so valuable?"

"I learned that something was on her mind or that she was planning something. If she had changed her behavior prior to her disappearance, then she wasn't kidnappcd or taken by surprise. Something was bothering her."

"That makes sense, I guess."

"It's one more piece of the puzzle."

"Are you any closer to finder her?"

"No," I admitted. "Not really."

# Chapter 20

Velda had a hankering for some authentic New England food so we invited Judy and Myra to join us for lunch at the Union Oyster House. Raw oysters as an appetizer didn't appeal to me, so I watched the other three as they made short work of the plate that the waiter put in front of us.

"You don't know what you're missing," exclaimed Myra as she picked up another oyster shell.

"I have a bowl of steamed clams coming. I like my shell fish cooked," I answered.

"Where's Rob?" asked Myra.

"I called him, but he's working a homicide case." I went on and told them about the shooting of the janitor and how it might or might not be related to Bishop Campbell's murder.

"Sounds like you have your hands full," remarked Myra.

"What about the missing girl?" asked Judy.

"Velda and I went to her school and talked to the head mistress. Something appeared to be on her mind the week before she disappeared.

"But you have a picture of her and the mystery girl, right?" asked Judy.

"I do, but they both look like every other teenage girl."

"May I see it?" asked Judy.

"Of course." I took the photograph from my coat pocket and handed it to her. She looked at it carefully and her expression changed. She then passed it to Myra, and Myra passed it to Velda. All three were staring at me.

"Men can be so stupid!" said Judy to the other two women. "You didn't notice anything unusual?" she asked me as Velda handed the photo back to me.

"It's just a picture of two young women who look alike. I don't see anything unusual."

"Sweetie," said Velda speaking to me as if I was a child. "It's not that they look alike that is so unusual. It's the fact that they are almost identical."

"Identical?"

"Look at the eyebrows," said Judy. "And the shape of the mouth, and the shape of the ears. They don't just look alike. Those two girls are related."

"I'll be damned," I said as I looked again at the photo.

The ladies decided to go shopping after lunch. I'd rather have a hot poker shoved into my entrails than shop with a group of women. I went back to Beacon Hill as I had a lot to think over.

If the two girls in the photo were related, that gave me a whole new range of possibilities. I'd have to check that out. I'd have to start with the father and see what he says. At least that was a lead.

My other two cases weren't looking as good. I had a murdered bishop, a missing quarter of a million dollars from the diocese, and a gambling janitor who had been shot. I had no idea how they were related. The bishop had been bashed over the head on his way to dinner with a person yet unknown. No leads beyond that.

My third case was almost as hopeless. I was working for the girlfriend of a phony medium who was discovered holding a pillow over the head of a dead woman. The only witness to the crime had an inconsistent story. Did she arrive and enter the house and see the murder, or was she already there? And how reliable was the old lady witness across the street?

"You got that scrunched up look on your face, Mr. Jeremy," observed Roscoe when he brought me in a hot cup of tea.

"I've got too many questions and not enough answers."

"You always come through in the end, Mr. Jeremy."

"I hope you're right, Roscoe."

I still wasn't convinced that the two girls were really related. As I've said before most teenage girls look alike. The fact that they have similar features could be a coincidence. I decided to have a little talk with the father and see if he had any ideas.

I rang the bell for Roscoe, which is not something I do very often. "Do you want to go out on a case with me?" I asked him.

"Absolutely!" he answered.

Ben Barrymore's office was located in downtown Boston, and I knew parking would be a problem and since it was less than half a mile, Roscoe and I bundled up against the cold and walked downtown.

The office was located in a ten story gray granite faced building that included a few art deco embellishments to break up the severity of the façade. The lobby had lots of tile and palm trees, and the elevator operator took us up to the top floor.

"Is Mr. Barrymore expecting you?" asked the receptionist seated behind a small switchboard.

"I don't have all day," I said as I handed her my card. She scurried off toward his office and quickly returned to usher us into his office.

"Mr. Dance, have you learned anything new about Marjorie?" He gave a glance at Roscoe.

"This is my assistant Mr. Jackson, and I do have a lead. Perhaps you could give me some information."

"Of course. What is it?"

I took out the photo and showed it to him. "Who is the other girl?"

"I've no idea," he said.

I decided to go with a hunch. "They look remarkably alike. Take another look. It's almost like they are sisters."

"Oh, my god!" Ben Barrymore's face lost all its color, and he seemed on the verge of fainting. Roscoe went to the water cooler and brought him back a glass of water. "Can I trust you to keep a secret?"

"I'm paid to keep secrets, Mr. Barrymore. Now if you have information that may help me find your daughter, you need to tell me."

"Let's go sit down over there," he said as he led us to a small sitting area in the corner of his office. He went to a small cabinet and poured out a three glasses of bourbon.

"When my wife was pregnant, I'm afraid I was indiscrete with my secretary at the time. Her name was Mildred Cousins. There was a child shortly after the birth of Marjorie. I paid for Mildred to go away to have the baby and sent her money every month for support. A few years later Mildred married, and the child was adopted. I never heard from her again after that.

"Then about two months ago I got a letter from a young woman who claimed to be the child. She asked if she could come and see me, but I didn't answer her. I thought it might be an attempt to blackmail me."

"Did she ask for money?"

"No."

"Did she ask for anything?"

"Only to meet me."

"Here's what I think may have happened. The girl wanted to connect with her real father. When you didn't respond she dug a little deeper into your life and discovered that she had a sister. She made contact with Marjorie and Marjorie was appalled by all this and sided with her sister. I think we'll find both of your daughters together,"

"Please, do anything you can."

"Do you know what the mother's married name is?"

"I believe it's Murdock."

"Do you know where she might be?"

"She settled in Providence, Rhode Island the last I heard."

"I'll see what I can do." I signaled to Roscoe that it was time to leave. "I'll check in with you in a few days."

Outside the building the wind had picked up and the temperature had dropped. I signaled for a taxi to take us back to Beacon Hill.

"Do you think you can find the missing girl?" asked Roscoe.

"I think I have a better chance now than I did a few hours ago."

"How did you figure it out?"

"It was the ladies who pointed out the fact that they might be related. To me all women look alike."

"Isn't that the truth," laughed Roscoe.

## Chapter 21

Velda had brought a new formality to the Beacon Hill Townhouse. She came down for dinner dressed in a blue evening gown with a matching shawl. She was adorned with a long string of pearls and blue sapphire earrings. Rob and I dressed up in white dinner jackets and pressed pants. Usually Rob and I would just eat from a tray in my study dressed in our work clothes.

We settled in the parlor for the cocktail hour. Velda stood by the fire holding a martini glass and looking a bit agitated.

"What's the matter?" I asked.

"Nothing really. I was just listening to the news on the radio, and they were talking about Germany. I made a lot of friends when I was in Berlin, and I worry about them." Velda downed her drink and went over to the bar and made herself another one.

"All eyes are on Germany right now," I said. "I'm sure Hitler doesn't want to piss off too many countries before the Summer Olympics."

"I don't think Hitler gives a shit about anything."

"Do any of them plan to leave Germany?" asked Rob.

"They all talked about it. I was the first to leave. Maybe the others will take my example."

"Most likely they will," I said. "Now if I'm not mistaken, I think dinner is ready." We went into the dining room. There were flowers and candles on the table. We were served by Roscoe, who had donned his best white outfit and had done a great job setting up the dinner.

"I thought you'd like to know that you ladies were right about the picture. It seems my client had an affair and an illegitimate daughter."

"What's this?" asked Rob. I filled him in about the similarity of the two girls. "Well. I missed that all together."

"The bottom line is that now I have the name of the other girl's mother and the fact that she lived in Providence at one time."

"So you might be able to find her?" asked Velda.

"I hope so."

"Well I have an announcement, too." said Rob. "I've been offered a job."

"A job doing what?" asked Velda before I could respond.

"A job as an insurance investigator. I'd be working by myself and wouldn't have to deal with the police higher-ups anymore."

"You'd give up homicide?" I asked.

"Yes, I think I would."

"Are you going to take it?" asked Velda.

"I need to think about it, but I'm inclined to take it."

"Does that mean I'd see you more often?" I asked.

"Every day, if you'd like."

"Yes, I'd like that very much."

Roscoe drove me to South Station to catch the morning train to Providence. Even sitting in first class the ride was tedious as we stopped at each little whistle stop along the way. It only took me a few minutes to read through the *Boston Post*, and then I had to entertain myself by looking out the window at the wintery landscape.

I came prepared to stay a few days because I had a feeling that finding Mildred Cousins Murdock might not be that easy, and even if I did find she might not know where her daughter was. The scenery continued to roll by, and I amused myself by watching my fellow travelers. Most everyone was dressed up without regard to the weather. I'd much rather be warm than fashionable.

The only times I been to Providence were on the train, and I never bothered to get off. I checked into the Biltmore Hotel, and I was pleased to see that city hall was right next door. That would save me some time at any rate.

Keeping in mind that I was spending Ben Barrymore's money and not my own, I took a modest room on the third floor. I slipped the bell hop a tip and unpacked before heading out to city hall.

The wind had picked up and even though city hall was a few yards away, I was frozen by the time I got there. I finally found the city clerk's office and was given the city directories for the past three years.

I started with the latest volume which was 1935. I found nothing for Mildred Murdock or Mildred Cousins. It was possible that she changed her name, but that wouldn't help me any. The 1934 volume was the same story, nothing. I hit pay dirt for 1933. I had the name of Mildred Murdock and an address. I copied down the information and headed back to the hotel for lunch.

I ordered a sandwich sent up to my room and reflected on the information I had. If there was no record of Mildred after 1933, what did that mean? Had she died? Moved away? Remarried? The only hope I had was to go to the address and see if I could find out any information.

I asked for directions at the front desk. The house was on the outskirts of town and more than likely was an apartment building. It was easy enough to find since it was a straight shot on the trolley out to that neighborhood.

It took me about ten minutes of walking around, but I finally found the gray triple decker. I read the names on the mailboxes, but there was no Murdock listed. I rang the bell to the first floor and I was in luck. A rather elderly woman came to the door. Elderly women, I had learned, loved to talk.

"May I help you?" She was dressed in a rather old fashioned dress and appeared to be about ninety.

"Good morning. My name is Jeremy Dance and I'm looking for Mildred Murdock."

"Oh dear! You better come in and sit down. Would you like some tea?"

"Yes, that would be lovely thank you." She scurried off to the kitchen and returned with tea and a plate of cookies.

"I'm afraid I have some bad news."

"Yes?"

"Mildred died some time ago."

"I see. What about her husband?"

"Anthony? I have no idea. He packed up and moved after his wife died. No word at all from him. What is it you're looking for?"

I explained the situation.

"Oh this is exciting! A real life detective on a case! Mr. Dance you are in luck."

"I am?"

"Yes! You see Debbie Murdock live upstairs on the third floor!"

# Chapter 22

It's been my experience that even the most bumbling fool can accidently stumble upon good luck. I was feeling lucky as I mounted the stairs to the third floor. I was feeling less lucky when I knocked at the door and got no answer. I looked at my watch and saw that it was only mid afternoon. Most likely the two girls were at work. I couldn't wait on the stairs for three hours, so I caught the trolley and went back to the hotel and took a nap.

I woke up around five and was hungry, but I wanted to get back to the apartment house and hopefully find Debbie Murdock and Marjorie Barrymore. I had to wait twenty minutes for the trolley and then stand for the entire trip as the car was full of workers heading home. I finally got to the triple decker, ran up the stairs, and knocked on the door. The door opened slightly with a security chain.

"Yes?" said the young woman. I could only see her partially, but I was pretty sure it was Marjorie Barrymore.

"I'd like to talk to you, Marjorie."

"How do you know my name?"

"I'm Jeremy Dance and your father hired me to find you."

"I'm not going back, so you can just forget it."

"I was hired to find you, not bring you back."

"Then you better come in, Mr. Dance," she said. She closed the door, took off the safety chain, and opened the door to admit me. I was taken into a small living room. Another young woman whom I took to be Debbie Murdock came into the room.

"This is Mr. Dance and he works for our father."

"I guess you were right," sighed Debbie. "He did have us tracked down."

"You don't sound surprised," I said to the two girls.

"My father only cares about his work. This was the only way I could get his attention," offered Marjorie.

"You better tell me the whole story."

"I'll let Debbie start." Debbie waved me to a seat and the two girls sat on the sofa.

"I was always told that I had been adopted by the Murdocks when I was two years old. When my mother died, my dad decided to go back to Kansas where he grew up. I had no wish to go to Kansas, so I remained here. I was only fifteen at the time and my aunt came to take care of me. She stayed with me until last June when I graduated from high school.

"I was going through my mother's papers when I came across my real birth certificate. Searching around, I found letters from Ben Barrymore and learned that he had paid support to my mother. I was excited to learn that I had a father, and I tried to contact him. He didn't answer my letters, and I couldn't reach him by phone.

"I decided to go to Boston. I wanted to at least see him, so I started following him around. When I learned he had a daughter I approached her and told her who I was." Here she stopped and Marjorie took over the narrative.

"You can imagine what a shock it was for me," said Marjorie taking a deep breath. "But the silver lining was that I had a sister. I'd been an only child and always dreamed of having a sister.

"When she told me that my father had refused to see her I was appalled. I couldn't go back to him knowing that he had a daughter he had cast off. My mother is dead and there is no reason that this couldn't come out in the open now. But I won't go back to that man knowing how cruel he is."

"You're not going to make her go back are you?" asked Debbie looking directly at me.

"Only if she wants to go back. But I do have to tell him I found her. But here's the situation as I understand it. Your father," I said to Debbie, "thought you were taken care of. He had no idea you had found out the truth. From what I gather he never received the letters because it all came as a surprise. This was an outright lie, but I figured it would be better to spare her feelings in this case.

"I didn't know where he lived, so I sent the letters to his office."

"A man like Ben Barrymore doesn't open his own mail. It's likely he never saw them. I'm going to give him a call when I get back to the hotel. It's very likely he's going to want both of you to come back. If that's the case would you go?"

Both the girls looked at each other and then nodded.

"Either way," I said. "I'll be back with news."

My phone call to Ben Barrymore was brief. I told him the story as the girls related it, and he was silent for a moment or two. "Tell me about the letters?" I demanded.

"I read the first one and thought it was a hoax. I gave my secretary orders to destroy any more that would arrive."

"For the sake of the girls' feelings, I think you might want to omit that part of the story," I suggested. "What do you want me to do?"

"I want you to bring them back."

Ben Barrymore was pacing back and forth on the platform at South Station as our train pulled in. Marjorie flew into his arms and Debbie approached him slowly. Ben held out his arm and the three of them shared an embraced.

One case down and two to go.

"So I really owe the three of you for helping me find the missing girl," I said. I had invited Judy, Myra, and Velda to lunch at the Ritz Carlton. I told them the story of my Providence adventure and added a few details in the spirit of good story telling.

"So Ben Barrymore accepted his illegitimate daughter into his family?' asked Myra. "I wonder if he would consent to a story?"

"From my last contact with him, he has decided that he wants to present Debbie as his daughter, though he doesn't quite know how to do it. I did suggest that you might help him craft a good cover story. Barrymore has rather significant investments in several newspapers, and I took the liberty of suggesting that any help you give him might be advantageous to your career."

"Oh Jeremy, you are a peach!" exclaimed Myra.

"Since you are in such a magnanimous mood," began Velda. "I'll take this opportunity to tell you I've arranged for a dinner party tomorrow."

"At my house I take it."

"You have no idea what tomorrow is, do you?" Judy and Myra were looking on with interest.

"Of course it's Friday."

"You see what I have to put up with?" Velda appealed to the other women. "It's our birthday you horse's ass!"

"Of course I knew that," I answered. I was bluffing. I had totally forgotten about it. I'd have to send Roscoe with some money to the jewelers as soon as I got home. All three women were shaking their heads and laughing. My bluff hadn't worked at all.

"So who's coming to this birthday dinner?" I asked.

"Our grandparents," she replied.

"Nonsense, they never come into the city." My grandparents had retired from the running of the department store and moved to Falmouth out on Cape Cod.

"Wrong dear brother. They're taking the train tomorrow and will be staying here at the hotel for a few days. You do realize we are turning twenty-eight tomorrow?"

"You're going to be a spinster," I said.

"And you'll be a confirmed bachelor."

# Chapter 23

The morning paper arrived and with it was the screaming headline: NO PROGRESS IN BISHOP'S DEATH! I was sure that Rob and the rest of the homicide department would be under a lot of pressure. I knew I would have to concentrate my efforts on the bishop's murder, but I also had to get back to work on Ruth Stone's murder.

Today, though, I needed to concentrate my efforts on family matters. I picked up the phone and called Tommy Beckford. Tommy had always liked my sister, and if he was still unattached, then he would make a good dinner companion for her.

Luck was with me because Tommy said he would be delighted to attend. Tommy worked as a lower functionary at one of the downtown banks, and I suspected that his life didn't involve many dinner parties.

Roscoe stood in the doorway waiting for me to get off the phone. "Yes Roscoe?"

"Everything is set for dinner tonight."

"Thank you, Roscoe. I'm sure it was difficult on such short notice. I'm afraid my sister is rather impulsive."

"I rather relish the challenge."

"And I know something else is on your mind."

157

"You did give me permission to hire someone to help out. I was hoping you could interview him. He's waiting downstairs."

"Is it James? The one you're been trying out?

"Yes, and I'd like to work with him."

"Bring him up, Roscoe. You've check his references?"

"Yes, sir. They are very impressive."

"Will he be living in?"

"Yes, sir. I've managed to clean up one of the rooms on the third floor where the old servant's rooms were."

"I have one more favor to ask. Would you be so kind as to run to the jewelry store on Arlington Street and find a nice little bauble for my sister's birthday?" I passed him a hundred dollars.

"That's going to be fun seeing their eyes when I present the money," said Roscoe laughing.

There was a knock on my study door. Jimmy Kirk appeared to be of Eurasian decent, was quiet, and seemed to be a good fit for the household.

"I make no apologies for the life that goes on here," I warned him. "But I do require discretion. Your previous references are very impressive, but I do not see references from your last employment."

"That is true, sir. I was let go by Mrs. Morrison when she discovered that I had a male visitor to my rooms."

"Mrs. Morrison is a narrow-minded bitch," I said. It was the first time Jimmy had smiled during the interview. "Just make sure your visitors use the back stairs. I'm not fond of meeting strangers in my house in the middle of the night."

"Then I have the job?"

"If you can bring me a cup of coffee in the next ten minutes, yes."

"Miss Pennington to see you," announced Roscoe. Myra practically flew into the room. Jimmy appeared with a pot of coffee and two cups.

"Good morning, Myra." I poured her a cup of coffee and passed it to her.

"I had dinner with Donna Jefferson last night."

"Ah, yes. Ruth Stone's niece."

"You asked me to let you know if I learned anything that might help in your investigation."

"What have you learned, Myra?" Was this the break in the case that I needed?

"Ruth Stone was going to change her will and leave her money to charity. She died before she could, however."

"You learned this from Donna?"

"Yes, I'm afraid that I may have encouraged her to overindulge in drink." I looked closely at Myra. There was more going on there than I had originally giver her credit for. "And I found this. I'm not sure if it's anything or not."

Myra passed me a piece of paper. It was a handwritten note that Ruth had written requesting a meeting with her lawyer.

"Myra, you are going to make one great investigative reporter!"

"How was your day?" I asked Rob as we dressed for dinner.

"The mayor wants some answers soon about Bishop Campbell's death."

"Something else is bothering you," I said looking directly at him.

"You remember when a police officer showed up here looking for me a few weeks ago?"

"Yes, I do."

"It seems my fellow homicide officers have found out I'm not just a poor lieutenant."

"I see."

"They're calling me the 'trust fund baby.'"

"But a very handsome one," I said taking his hand. He smiled.

Roscoe came running into the room. "Taxi just arrived."

"It must be my grandparents. Courage everyone!" I put on my dinner jacket and rushed downstairs.

"Grandfather, you look elegant," I said as I shook his hand. "And Granny, you look wonderful."

"Liar!" said my grandmother, but she smiled and offered her cheek for a kiss.

"Your grandmother gets more beautiful with age," said the old man.

"Good evening everyone," said Velda as she descended the stairs. She was dressed in a yellow gown with an emerald necklace that really showed off her healthy complexion. "So good to see you both," she said as she gave them a hug. We all went into the parlor where Jimmy was mixing drinks.

"So I understand you're calling yourself Dance now," said my grandfather to me.

"So is Velda. I hope you don't mind," I answered. "I'd rather not be associated with my father."

"Not at all. They only thing good he ever did was give us grandchildren," said my grandmother. "We begged your mother, may she rest in peace, not to marry him. And that harpy of a stepmother you ended up with should be locked up."

"No argument from us," added Velda.

Rob stood attentively in the doorway. "This is Robert Williams," I said as I waved him in.

"Come here and let me look at you," commanded my grandmother. "Now I see why my grandson finds you so attractive. This man is a work of art." Rob turned bright red.

"You're embarrassing him," I said.

"If I was forty years younger I'd do more than embarrass him," she laughed.

"Easy old woman," offered my grandfather laughing.

Shortly thereafter the rest of the guests arrived. Tommy Beckford began flirting with Velda right away. Judy and Myra had tried to outdo each other in choosing gowns for the evening. Velda gave me gold and ruby cufflinks for my birthday and I gave her emerald earrings.

My grandfather presided over dinner and entertained us with stories from the department stores. Velda and I had heard the stories before, but we always found them entertaining.

"And Jeremy, tell us about your latest case," said my grandfather.

I told the group as best I could without giving names. Of course the bishop's death was public record, and I had no need to protect my clients for that case. I didn't tell them about the missing money. The money may or may not be part of the case.

"I understand," began my grandfather when I finished, "that we lost a rent paying business in the downtown building the business owns. You requested a termination of The Tabard's lease?"

"I did, indeed."

"Care to tell me why we're losing rental income?" All the eyes were on me.

"I didn't like their attitude," I said and then went on to tell them about how Roscoe and I were treated.

"Not to mention," cut in Rob, "that a man was shot dead in the bar that same night."

"Then you did the right thing," said my grandmother, coming to my defense. We can't have that can we, Henry?"

"No, we can't, dear," replied my grandfather.

We were all a little startled when the lights went out until Roscoe entered with a birthday cake alight with twenty-eight candles.

"The cake is beautiful," gushed my sister. In truth it was highly decorated. "What bakery did you find this?"

"Jimmy Kirk did it," Roscoe said simply.

"It's amazing," I said. "But please, no one sing 'Happy Birthday.'"

And no one did.

Ralph O'Reilly stood in front of my desk shifting his weight back and forth from one leg to another. Clearly he had too much energy. O'Reilly was one of the top forgers in the business. Having served a rather lengthy prison term for forgery, he now freelanced as a consultant on forgery.

"I need you to forge a document for me," I said.

"I don't do that no more."

"Sure you don't." I passed him a roll of money.

"I want you to create a work of fiction. I want you to create a will and make it look like it was written in the hand of this woman." I passed him the note Myra had brought me in the hand writing of Ruth Stone. "I am not going to use it in a crime."

"As long as you ain't going to use it for criminal activity, I guess it would be okay."

"Can you have it ready by tomorrow?"

"Sure thing."

# Chapter 24

**B**etty Bronson sat nervously in the red leather chair in my study. "Have you found out anything yet? Ramon is still in jail. His trial begins next week. If they find him guilty..." she just shivered.

"I have some new information. If I'm right Ramon will be out of jail in a few days."

"You believe him then?"

"I'm afraid I do. But I don't approve of what the two of you were doing."

"I know,' she said simply. "Ramon feels he does have a gift, but it's unpredictable. When his gift isn't working, he's had to make stuff up so not to disappoint his clients." That was the story she was selling, but I wasn't buying.

"So how did you get involved in all this?" I was curious.

"Back home in Vermont there's been a lot of interest in spiritualism. We lost a lot of men in the war. My brother died in the Argon Forest." Her eyes filled with tears, and she looked away. "Ramon came to town and offered a séance. During the séance my brother came through. He said things that only I would know. I was impressed and stayed after the séance to talk with Ramon. We hit it off and at the end of the week I left with him. We've been together ever since."

I was feeling somewhat less disgusted by Ramon Decamp, but not a lot.

"You're taking a big risk," said Rob when I told him my plan.

"So?"

"I'm just warning you that it could all backfire on you if you're wrong."

"Well, I've heard that Argentina is a lovely country in which to live."

"I guess we could do with a change of scenery. I've always wanted to visit there."

"I'm confident I'm on the right track."

"I hope you're right."

"If we find out that Ramon didn't kill Ruth Stone, will the district attorney file charges for fraud?"

"Not a chance."

"How come?"

"It would be impossible to prove. You can't really prove that spirits don't exist in a court of law, especially considering how many people believe in it. Unless one of his victims wants to pursue criminal intent, then there's nothing we can do, and here's the surprising thing, that little group you were in doesn't want to press charges. In fact I think they still half believe he's the real thing."

"Well, there's an end of it I guess."

I called Donna Jefferson and asked her to come to my office. I told her I just needed to put the finishing touches on my files and give her a final copy of the records. She agreed to come.

"Good morning Mr. Dance," Donna Jefferson said as she entered my office."

"Have a seat, Miss Jefferson," I indicated the red chair. "I understand congratulations are in order."

"How so?"

"It seems you've inherited a large sum of money."

"Yes, but poor Aunt Ruth," she said a squeezed out a tears. "I'd rather have her back than the money."

"Drop the act, Donna. You're not that good an actress."

"How dare you," she said. Rage filled her face.

"I've something here you should look at." I reached into my top drawer and pulled out a sheet of paper. Ralph O'Reilly had done a very good job imitating Ruth Stone's handwriting. I passed it to her.

"What's this?" she asked as she scanned the paper.

"It's the revised will Ruth Stone wrote two days before she died. Notice the handwriting and the date. Also notice that you have been completely cut out of the will."

"What do you want?" I took the paper out of her hands and put it back in the top drawer.

"Ten thousand dollars to start, and Ruth's revised will goes away. Otherwise being the good citizen that I am, I'll have to turn it over to the courts."

"I hate you."

"I don't much care. Looks like you killed your aunt for nothing."

"Yes, and I'll kill you, too." She started fumbling in her purse for a gun.

"Put the purse down," said Rob, holding a gun to her head. He had been standing behind an oriental screen in the corner of my office.

"I'll deny everything," she said.

"We have three witnesses that just heard you admit to killing your aunt and threatening to kill Mr. Dance," replied Rob. Roscoe Jackson stepped out from behind the screen. "Donna Jefferson, I'm arresting you for the murder of Ruth Stone." Two police matrons entered my office and slapped the handcuffs on Donna Jefferson and took her away.

"Looks like my little ruse worked," I said. I took the forged will and threw it in the fire.

"Yes, it did," admitted Rob.

Now that I had finally finished with Ruth Stone's murder and the disappearance of Marjorie Barrymore, I could devote all my energies on Bishop Campbell's murder. I had half hoped that the police would come up with a lead and solve the case, but so far they hadn't made any more progress than I had.

Roscoe was serving me breakfast as I was perusing the morning paper when a headline caught my eye:

### Father Reunited with Missing Daughter after Seventeen Years

by Myra Pennington

Investment banker Benjamin Barrymore has been reunited with his missing daughter Deborah after seventeen years. Deborah was one of two daughters born to Mr. Barrymore and his late wife. The disappearance of the child was believed to have been a kidnapping. A ransom note was found and a warning not to contact the police or the child would be killed. Mr. Barrymore periodically paid the ransom, but never contacted the police for fear of injury to the child. Over the years Mr. Barrymore hired private investigators, but to no avail. Last week the well-known Beacon Hill agent, Jeremy Dance, was able to locate the missing girl and reunite her with her family.

Apparently Myra was able to write a good cover story to conceal the fact that Barrymore had an affair and an illegitimate daughter. It was a good story, and I was sure Myra would be rewarded with a sudden career advancement. It also was a good advertisement for my services, though I hoped I wouldn't have any more cases for a few weeks.

## Chapter 25

Rob had been moping about the house for two days. He had been given full credit for the arrest of Ruth Stone's murderer, so I couldn't understand what was bothering him.

"You've been too quiet," I said finally on the second day. "What's the matter?"

"Nothing really, just a lot on my mind."

"You just solved a major murder case."

"No, you just solved a murder case."

"Doesn't matter to me."

"I know, but a woman is till dead and another one is going to prison."

"It's more than that, so spill the beans."

"The department is getting pressure to solve the bishop's murder, and I'm afraid that if we don't get the truth soon, the higher ups are going to demand we make something up."

"They'd do that?"

"Oh, yes they would. It's a black eye on the department that we haven't been able to solve the murder of a clergyman."

"But as far as the public knows the death is suspicious, it hasn't been officially released as a homicide."

"That's the only thing in our favor at the moment."

"Well, I intend to devote myself full time on the case, now that I don't have any other cases at the moment. But I know you and there's more to the story."

"I've been thinking of the job offer."

"Becoming an insurance investigator instead of a homicide cop?"

"Yes, I'm torn. I love being a cop, but I hate taking orders and having to keep a schedule."

"So I'm hearing one positive for the cop job, and two negatives."

"Well, I never thought of it that way."

"Both are good jobs, so you'll win either way. As soon as we resolve the bishop's murder, one way or another, let's plan a little trip. We can go away for a few weeks and when we get back you'll have a better perspective."

"Yes, that's a great idea."

"Now cheer up and let's go to the club for lunch."

Lunch at the Windsor Club was always an event. Rob had to limit himself to one drink since he had to go on duty in the evening. It seems that there are more murders at night than in the morning.

"So let's look at what we have so far in the bishop's murder," I suggested.

"The bishop's body was discovered in the late evening outside the Windsor Club by the club's chef. The bishop was a member of the club. He most likely had just left the club, but no one seems to know. Lyle Compton, the manager, was the second person to know about the death and then he called you," Rob had taken out his notebook to make sure that he had his facts in order.

"Lyle Compton,' I replied, "was worried about bad publicity and called me in. It was I who told him to call you directly. It appeared to us that he died of a massive head wound. We surmised that it wasn't self inflected or the result of an accident. That was later confirmed by the medical examiner.

"In order to allow more time for an investigation, we allowed the newspapers to report the death as a probable accident. Word leaked out to the press that the death may have been suspicious. Right now we have a ticking time bomb where any minute the press may decide to print the story as a possible homicide."

"Do you think there's any way we can get *The Boston Post* to hold off on the story?" asked Rob.

"Isn't the editor a member of this club? I've seen him here."

"If he is, we may be able to convince him to hold off."

"Let's talk to Lyle Compton after lunch," I suggested. "He'll know for sure."

"Good idea. What other things about the case do we know?"

"We checked his apartment and didn't find anything."

"Didn't you find a paper or something?"

"Just a paper with random words on it. More importantly we noticed that his appointment book was missing."

"And it was found in the men's room at the club behind the toilet tank. The question then is why did the bishop hide it? We looked at it, and it really didn't have anything in it that we could decipher."

"Maybe the bishop didn't hide the book, maybe the killer did," said Rob.

"We do know that the bishop was on his way to Gibby's Restaurant and that he had reserved a table for two. We also know that neither of them showed up, so the most likely scenario is that he was killed by whoever he was meeting for dinner."

"And the motive?" asked Rob.

"There was the choir director who was fired after a scandal back in the Midwest. The bishop was somehow involved with him."

"Should we track him down?"

"We should at least see if he was anywhere near Boston at the time of the bishop's murder." I didn't think it likely, but maybe we were on to something. "Don't forget why the bishop was here in Boston."

"He was here to help raise funds, right?"

"And to find out why a quarter of a million dollars was missing from the diocese."

"So either money or revenge?" stated Rob.

"It could be love or jealousy, too. We haven't even looked at that."

"Where did you get that?" asked Rob.

"His appointment book. He seemed to have a regular appointment with someone noted in his book as SM."

"Well, I guess we have some leads to follow, but right now I want to concentrate on this lovely piece of sirloin on my plate," said Rob as he dug into his lunch.

Our meeting with Lyle Compton revealed the fact the Ed Hynes, the editor of the *Boston Post* was indeed a member of the Windsor Club. Lyle checked the log books and told me when Hynes was most likely to be at the club. It seemed he had a regular schedule, which was very helpful for me.

Rob went off to get ready for work. I had a few hours to kill before Hynes was due to show up at the club. The Windsor Club had a very good reading room, so I grabbed a couple of books off the shelf and glanced through them waiting for Ed Hynes to appear. I had a hard time reading because something kept nagging at me about the bishop's apartment. Rob and I had gone through it and not found anything helpful, but I kept feeling that I might have missed something.

I had a fairly good idea what Hynes looked like, though I had never formally met him. It was about four in the afternoon when he strolled into the reading room. I let him settle down in a chair before I approached him.

"Mr. Hynes?"

175

"Yes?"

"I'm Jeremy Dance," I passed him my card and we shook hands.

"Hello, Mr. Dance, I've seen you around the club."

"I wonder if we might talk."

"Of course," he answered and gestured for me to take the chair next to his. "What can I do for you?"

"You are familiar with the untimely death of Bishop Campbell here in Boston?"

"Yes, and I suspect the public hasn't been told the entire truth. Terrible business."

"I've been hired by a certain party to find the truth about the bishop's death."

"I have heard of you Mr. Dance. May I ask who you represent?'

"I cannot divulge my clients. They hire me to keep their names out of the papers."

"Of course, but I don't understand what that has to do with me."

"*The Boston Post* has been hinting that the murder of the bishop was suspicious. It's important that the police be allowed to investigate without public pressure. It's also important that my clients be protected.

"It would make a huge difference if you could hold off on public speculation until we have finished the investigation," I said.

"I sell newspapers because I report the news." Ed Hynes was looking slightly angry.

176

"As you know the bishop's body was found just outside the club. The bishop was a member here, as are you. You are well aware that for this club to exist, we have to keep it exclusive and private. We don't need reporters discovering who our members are and what our mission here is."

"I've kept my reporters away from the club," Hynes responded.

"You're not the only newspaper in town. If you start stirring up interest, your rivals will be all over us."

"I suppose that's true."

"So here's the deal. Drop the story. Report that the death was accidental. In return when all the facts are known, your newspaper will get an exclusive."

"How do I know you're telling the truth?"

"First of all I get my business through referrals from people I've helped. Double crossing a powerful editor of a major newspaper would not be in my best interest. Second of all, your reporter, Myra Pennington, is a friend of mine. I'd like to help her career by giving her the story."

"I think, Mr. Dance, we can do business." We shook hands. "Would you care to join me for a drink?"

"Thank you, I'd love a drink."

# Chapter 26

The beginning of February in Boston had been cold and stormy, but as Valentine's Day came and went the weather had warmed up slightly and the days were noticeable longer. March in New England is the stormy month when winter and spring fight a death duel, so I knew that the nice weather wouldn't last. As the sidewalks cleared and the pavement dried, I found myself walking more and more. It was good exercise, but it also helped to clear my head.

I'd need a clear head if I was to help find the killer of Bishop Campbell.

"What are you doing today?" asked Rob as he stepped out of the shower and began drying himself off with a towel.

"I'm meeting with Bishop Anderson and his staff. I'm hoping to track down who this mysterious SM is that Campbell met with on a regular basis."

"Do you think that might be the killer? Because most likely he or she isn't."

"It will help me know more about the bishop. I think the more information I have, the better chance I have in stumbling over the answer. How are the police doing?"

"Since the newspapers have dropped the story, the pressure is off and I'm afraid that it's dropped down the priority list."

"Just as I thought."

"Fortunately you are still on the case," said Rob with a wink.

"Yes, I get to do the work and you get the credit. Now get dressed, breakfast is in twenty minutes, and Velda doesn't like to eat alone.

The three men were waiting for me as I entered the bishop's office. Bishop Anderson indicated a seat. I sat and faced Archdeacon Peter Ramsey, Canon Tim Black, and the bishop.

"I've been able to persuade the newspapers to drop the story for the time being. I've also arranged to have a reporter I trust handle the story. I should be able to provide some measure of control to protect the diocese as much as possible."

"Thank you, Mr. Dance. I'm sure we all appreciate it," responded the bishop. The look on Tim Black's face was anything but grateful.

"Have you any new clues?" asked the archdeacon.

"Right now the police are investigating the death of your janitor. It may or may not be related but it does seem a coincidence that there have been two deaths in one workplace, both by violence."

"But we know Bill Rogers was a gambler," said Tim Black.

"I don't have any solid evidence yet as to his gambling problem." I looked straight at Black until he was forced to look away. "Anyway, a lead I want to follow up on comes from his appointment book. He had a meeting with someone he referred

179

to as SM almost every Monday. Do you happen to know who that would be?"

All three looked at each other and shook their heads.

"Perhaps then you can give me some idea of Bishop Campbell's activities in Boston. Anything you can think of. I know he was involved in fund raising. But whom did he work for? Did he work at any of the local churches? What was his spiritual life like?"

"Well," began the archdeacon, "he was the chaplain to the Sisters of St. Columba."

"The Episcopal nuns?" I asked.

"Yes, they have a convent at Louisburg Square," added the bishop. I had often seen the nuns hurrying down Beacon Hill to the Church of the Advent.

"Could you arrange a meeting for me with the Mother Superior?" I asked the bishop.

"I'll call over there right now if you like," said the bishop, and he went to the outer office and placed a call.

"Anything else the two of you could add?" I asked Archdeacon Ramsey and Canon Black.

"Sorry if I seem a little impatient," confessed Black. "Mr. Rogers, the janitor, worked for me and I feel responsible. Please find out who killed him."

"I'll do my best."

"The sisters will be expecting you, Mr. Dance. You may meet with them this afternoon."

"Thank you. We shook hands all around and I headed out to meet Velda for lunch.

"Why ever did you want to have lunch here?" I asked Velda as I took a seat in the booth. Velda had suggested that we have lunch in the Dance Department Store tea room.

"In case you forgot, we will probably own this store one day."

"Or sell it," I said.

"Or sell it," she agreed. "Anyhow the food is good and the service is outstanding."

"Of course the service is outstanding. They all know who we are. Anyway I almost expected to see Tommy Beckford here."

"Not a chance. Last time I took you to lunch with a boy, he ended up doing unspeakable things with you," she laughed.

"Better you know about them up front than be surprised later."

"I guess that's true," she sighed.

"So something is on your mind, isn't it?"

"You know I love staying at your house."

"And you can stay at my house as long as you like," I said.

"That's just it," she answered. "It's your house. I want to have my own place."

"Are you still planning to set up a studio in Maine?"

"In the summer, yes. But I want to have a place in town. I want to be near you."

"And Tommy Beckford," I'm sure."

"I don't know if Tommy and I will hit it off or not. But if we do I'd like to have some privacy."

We had to pause in our conversation when our meals arrived.

"I understand," I said. "In fact I'll help you find a place."

"Thank you. For a brother, you're pretty nice.'

"Don't you dare," I said laughing, "threaten my reputation."

I arrived promptly at two o'clock at the convent. Louisburg Square was the most exclusive neighborhood in the very exclusive Beacon Hill section of Boston. I didn't know much about the convent, but I guessed that a rich benefactor had left the building to them, along with a substantial endowment for its upkeep.

I rang the bell and was admitted by a nun in a gray habit who ushered me into a small reception room. The room was richly detailed, but the furnishings were solid, but simple. I was left to my own amusement for a few minutes before another nun came in.

"I'm Sister Mary, the superior. I understand you are looking into the death of Bishop Campbell. Such a tragic accident. Please sit down, Mr. Dance."

"I'm sorry to say, sister, but the bishop's death was no accident."

"But I thought that was all just a rumor. Oh, dear."

"I understand that the bishop was the chaplain for the convent?"

"Oh yes," she said. I could tell I'd have to lead the conversation.

"I've been hired by the diocese to look into the death. It would be extremely helpful if you can tell me anything whether you think it is related or not. I'm casting a wide net, hoping to catch a clue. When did you first meet the bishop?"

"We had been friends since childhood. He was somewhat older than I, but he lived across the street from me when I was growing up in Wisconsin."

"Do you happen to know if there was someone in his life he referred to by the initials SM? It seems that he met with him once a week, and…" She held up her hand to stop me.

"I'm SM; that is Sister Mary. We met for tea every Monday." I felt rather stupid not to have made that connection.

"Do you know what he was working on?" I asked. She looked torn, as if she wanted to tell me something, but held back. "The bishop is dead. Any promise you made to him is rendered null."

"He told me that money had disappeared from the diocese account. He was investigating it. You don't think that's why he was killed."

"It is possible," I answered. "Do you know what he was investigating?"

"All he said was that he was close to an answer, though I got the feeling that he wasn't too happy about what he had found out."

"Thank you sister. You've been a big help," I said as I got up to leave.

"I do hope so," said the sister softly.

## Chapter 27

Jimmy Kirk had blended seamlessly into the household. A quiet an efficient worker, he freed Roscoe from some of the more mundane tasks and allowed him to devote more of his time as my assistant.

"Roscoe, I think we have to establish whether Bill Rogers getting shot is at all related to Bishop Campbell's murder."

"Do you think there's a connection?"

"If there is then we are looking for something much bigger, and we might be able to gather a few more clues. If not, then we'll be no further ahead."

"What would you like me to do?"

"You have friends who have friends who gamble, don't you?" I asked Roscoe.

"And you want me to ask around and see what I can find out about Bill Rogers?

"Exactly."

Aiden Brookfield and Thomas Masson were two strikingly handsome real estate men who had agreed to show Velda and me some Beacon Hill properties. Since they were good friends of mine, I knew I would have personal care and not be shuffled off to one of their lesser agents.

Aiden and Tom were waiting for us at a townhouse on Acorn Street.

"Thank you for helping us," said Velda as the two greeted us.

"Not at all," said Thomas.

The façade of the house was brick and seemed to blend in with the other townhouses on the block. The only distinguishing features were the blue door and the polished brass door knocker. Aiden unlocked the door, and we stepped inside a hallway. The house was vacant and in need of a good cleaning.

"The first floor has a parlor and a dining room. The kitchen is in the back. Upstairs on the second floor are three rooms and another large room on the third floor," said Thomas as he led us into the parlor. There was a fireplace and double pocket doors that opened into the dining room.

"It's rather small," I said looking around.

"It's perfect," said Velda. "I don't need a house as big as yours."

"Wait until you see the backyard," said Aiden and he led us through the dining room into the kitchen and out to the back porch. The yard was walled in and looked like it would be a great place to spend a summer afternoon.

"Let's all go to lunch," suggested Velda, "And talk about the details, because I think I want to buy this place."

Roscoe was mixing martinis when Velda and Judy returned from an afternoon of shopping. Rob had just returned from finishing his shift at the police station, and we were gathered in the parlor by the fire.

"I heard you might buy a house," said Rob to Velda.

"Actually I put a deposit on it this afternoon. I got it for a great price."

"Are you sure you don't want to look around?" I asked.

"I love the place. No need to look further."

"She took me to see it before we came here," added Judy. "It's a cute little neighborhood."

"I'll miss you," said Rob.

"No you won't. You'll have my brother all to yourself," she laughed sipping her martini.

"Anything new on the Bill Rogers shooting?" I asked Rob.

"Nothing yet. How about you?"

"I've asked Roscoe to look up some friends of his friends in the gambling world and see if anyone knows anything." Roscoe looked up and nodded as he refilled our glasses.

"Why are you looking into a bar room shooting?" asked Judy.

"It might have a bearing on the bishop's case," I answered.

"Dinner is served," announced Jimmy Kirk as he stood in the doorway.

"Drink up everyone," I said as we headed o the dining room.

Dinner was a hearty seafood chowder with biscuits. Jimmy had taken over much of the cooking, and his cooking was almost equal to Roscoe's. Everyone exclaimed over the food. When Roscoe came in to clear the dishes away I said, "You can tell Jimmy his probationary period is over; He has a job."

"Yes sir, Mr. Jeremy."

Jimmy appeared smiling with a chocolate cake for dessert.

"If it's okay with you Mr. Jeremy, I'll take the night off and get started on the assignment you gave me," said Roscoe as he cleared some dishes out of the way.

"Here's something to gamble with. I'll expect you to split the winnings with me." I reached in my pocket and got my wallet out.

"Yes sir," he said as he took the money and left for the evening.

We sat back and looked at the remains of the chocolate cake.

"I never want to eat again," said Judy as she sipped her coffee.

"What shall we do this evening?" asked Velda.

"Let's listen to the radio,' suggested Rob.

"That's fine," I said. "As long as it's not a murder mystery. I've had enough of them already.

The murder of Ruth Stone had made a sensation when the facts were known. Donna Jefferson's trial was put on the fast track by the district attorney's office. I suspected the district attorney had some political aspirations since this trial was getting a lot of publicity. This case had everything that reporters dream of: spiritualism, fraud, greed, a will, and a pretty murderess.

Both Rob and I were the key witnesses. While my name was familiar only to a very small group of Bostonians, one enterprising reporter had discovered my little business and began to refer to me in print as "The Restorer."

I wasn't sure if the added publicity would bring in new business or not, but I was prepared to think so.

The trial took place in four days. Rob and I sat in the courtroom until we were called as witnesses. I was called first and gave my story. Rob was called next. Agnes Parker, the neighbor across the street, testified that Donna had not left the house that day.

The defense tried to cast doubts on our testimony, but in the end it took the jury only three hours to convict Donna Jefferson of first degree murder.

As soon as the news of the conviction hit the paper I was offered several cases. Unfortunately they were divorce cases, and I had no interest in inserting myself into peoples' marital problems. Another case proved more interesting. It was a chance to track down a missing heir to a small annuity, however when I stated my monetary requirements, the party lost interest.

I was sitting in the parlor having my morning coffee and reading the newspaper. The major story was the sentencing of Donna Jefferson. She was destined to spend many years in prison.

"Gentleman to see you, Mr. Jeremy," said Roscoe as he came into the room.

"It's a bit early, Roscoe," I said as I looked at the clock. It was nine o'clock; I guessed the gentleman was a professional who was used to punctuality. "Send him in I guess."

The man came into the room wearing a navy blue pinstripe suit carrying his hat in his hand. "Forgive the early intrusion, Mr. Dance. I wonder if we might talk in confidence. My name is Henry Stanton."

"Have a seat Mr. Stanton." I indicated the red chair. "What can I do for you?"

"I've seen your name in the papers, and I've made several inquiries. I understand that you find lost items."

"What have you lost Mr. Stanton?"

"Oh, it's not me that's lost something, Mr. Dance. You see, I'm the curator of the Langley Museum. We're missing a few items."

"The Langley is a small museum of modern art isn't it?"

"Yes, it is. Have you been there?"

"Yes, I have, Mr. Stanton. What is it you are missing?"

"We're missing a jade vase and a small painting by Miro."

190

"When did they go missing?"

"That's just it, we don't know."

"You don't know?"

"We have much of our collection in storage. When we did an inventory yesterday we discovered them missing."

"How much are they worth?"

"They are insured for one hundred and fifty thousand, but of course they are priceless."

I'd seen Miro's works and didn't classify them as priceless, but then again I wasn't a curator. "Why not just collect the insurance?"

"We would rather have the art back. It's part of an exhibition we're putting on later this year."

"What would you like me to do for you, Mr. Stanton?"

"Find the art."

"In order to find the art I have to find out who took it." I passed him a list of my consulting fees. He didn't flinch.

"Does that mean you'll do it?"

"I should warn you I'm working on a murder case at the moment, so I won't be able to devote all my time to your case."

"Understood."

"I'll be at your office tomorrow about nine then." We shook hands and Henry Stanton got up to go.

## Chapter 28

Velda buttered her toast and looked across the breakfast table at me. "You took on another case?"

"Yes, I think it's going to be an easy one."

"Why do you say that?"

"They are distinctive pieces of art. They'll be hard to fence. And what about you? Have you chosen a moving date yet?"

"I'm meeting with the real estate boys today. The house is just perfect. I can make the third floor into a studio."

"You haven't done any painting since you've been here."

"I know; that's why I need to set up my studio as soon as possible."

Jimmy Kirk came into the dining room bringing more coffee. "Where's Roscoe?" I asked.

"He left early this morning. He said to tell you that he has a lead," replied Jimmy.

"I hope so. I need something to move this case."

"Where's Rob?" asked Velda.

"I suspect he's out on a case. We'll probably see him tonight."

"Not me," said Velda. "I'll be out with Tommy Beckford."

"Do I hear wedding bells?"

"Don't be funny. But things are going well in that direction."

"You could do worse."

"So could he."

"Have you slept with him yet?"

"Sometimes, Jeremy, you say the most shocking things."

"I'll take that as a yes. This is the twentieth century you know. No need to be prudish."

"Easier for men," said Velda. She got up, patted me on the head, and went to change.

I found out that the Langley Museum had moved from its previous small building to a converted warehouse on outer Massachusetts Avenue. The first thing I did was circle the building, looking for an entry points that might make getting inside the museum easy. The loading dock on the back was sealed up and the windows were high off the ground. The whole museum was visible from all sides so that any attempted entry would most likely be seen by someone.

I found Henry Stanton in his office waiting for me. We got the polite greetings out of the way, and he indicated a chair for me to sit down on.

"How many people do you have who work here?" I asked.

"Only ten. We are not a large museum."

"And how many volunteers?"

"Eight at last count."

"How many former workers or volunteers?"

"I'd have to check the files to answer that. You think it was someone connected to the museum?"

"It's something worth checking out," I answered. I didn't want to alarm him by telling him that a lot or art theft is by someone in a position of trust. "A good place for me to start is with your employee files."

"I'll have my secretary bring them to you. I've an extra office you can use for the time being."

"Then I might as well get started."

I sat going through the personnel files and the volunteers' application. Most of them seemed unremarkable, but there were four files that I put aside to take a closer look later. At lunch I went to a drugstore around the corner and had a sandwich at the lunch counter. Then it was time to hop on the trolley and return home.

Even before I could get through the front door I could tell that Roscoe had something on his mind. He took my jacket and hat from me without a word, but he was bouncing from one foot to the other as if he had too much energy.

"What is it, Roscoe?"

"I got some news about the janitor fellow."

"Let's go into the study and have a seat before you wear a hole in the floor." I indicated the red chair and Roscoe tried to fit his large frame in it.

"I have a friend Willie who gambles," said Roscoe.

"I don't doubt it," I replied.

"Willie plays poker. It seems that he knows this Mr. Rogers. Willie said he's a big player and, he loses all the time."

"That at least confirms that Rogers was a gambler."

"There's more. Willie says this Rogers was bragging that he was onto something big. Something that would pay off."

"Good work, Roscoe."

"This Mr. Rogers said he had some information that someone was going to pay him to keep to himself."

"Blackmail? Excellent! Now we have a motive for the shooting. When Rob comes home, I want you to tell him what you told me."

"I can't get Willie in trouble. He doesn't trust white folk."

"Don't worry, Roscoe. We aren't concerned with Willie's gambling. And Roscoe..."

"Yes?"

"Thanks!"

Rob came home in time to shower and change for dinner. I told him about Roscoe's discovery as he was changing.

"At least we have a motive for murder," he said as he was fiddling with his cufflinks.

"Here, let me help you," I said as I took the cufflinks out of his hand. "We have the motive and you've talked to the witnesses. Anything new there?"

"All the witnesses say the same thing. The bar was dark, and a man took out a gun and shot Rogers. The man was wearing an oversized coat and trousers. Nobody saw his face."

"Oversize coat and trousers?"

"That's right."

"Then it probably wasn't the killer's own clothes. Who goes around wearing too big trousers?"

I had a sudden thought. "Could it have been a woman dressed as a man?"

"I suppose," said Rob. "Whoever it was they were being blackmailed."

"Let's go down to dinner,' I suggested. "I think we're eating alone."

"Where's Velda?"

"Out with Tommy Beckford."

"So I have you all to myself tonight?"

"And then some," I replied.

The next morning I was up early and happened to be at the top of the stairway when I heard Velda come in.

"Sneaking in after a night of shameless hedonism?"

"I'm not sneaking in, I'm walking in boldly."

"Good for you. Are you hungry?"

"Starving!"

"The least Tommy could have done was take you out to breakfast."

"The lazy bum is still asleep. He took all the covers, too."

"Just keep that in mind for when it gets serious."

"Don't worry; I'll give him some direction."

"I don't doubt it."

"Where's Rob?"

"He left early for work," I explained.

"It seems like he only comes here to sleep."

"Busy life."

"What are you doing today?"

"I'm going to work on my two cases and have lunch with Judy. Would you like to come?"

"Where?"

"We're having lunch at the St. Regis."

"I think I will join you. Haven't been there in years."

"Okay, see you at one."


I looked across the desk to Henry Stanton. "I'm convinced that whoever stole the art works either works here or used to work here."

"That's a disturbing thought."

"What can you tell me about these four people?" I placed the four folders on his desk. He looked at them carefully and frowned.

"John Roux left the museum several weeks ago to take up a job in San Francisco. I don't think he could sneak into the museum without being seen and I know that he's still in San Francisco?"

"How?"

"I got a letter from him yesterday."

"How about this one?"

"Steven Templeton?" He's one of our part time curators."

"Part time? That doesn't sound financially rewarding," I said.

"No. In fact he's complained about his reduced hours for some time. We had to cut costs you know. Art is the first casualty of a stock market turn down." I thought probably that the poor were the first casualties, but I kept that thought to myself.

"Is he here now?" I asked.

"No, this is one of his days off."

"Could I see his office?"

"I'll take you there myself."

Stanton led me into a small office with gray walls, a filing cabinet, and a desk and chair. The room was unremarkable in every aspect, except the file cabinet seemed too big for the room. I checked the drawers of the desk and found only a supply of ink, pens, and blotters.

Stanton was standing in the doorway watching me. "Not finding anything?"

"The desk seems clean. Where did the office furniture come from?"

"Just standard equipment from an office supply store," Stanton gave me a quizzical look.

"It's just that the file cabinet seems somehow out of place."

"Oh that. Steve Templeton brought that in himself. He said he needed more file storage. He said the one we bought for the office wasn't big enough."

"I think we need to take a closer look at Mr. Templeton," I said as I started opening file drawers. I wasn't finding anything unusual in the files.

"Why do you say that?"

"If you look closely at the file drawers, you'll notice that they seem a little short for such a deep file cabinet."

"So?"

"So help me move this cabinet around." He grabbed one side, and I grabbed the other, and we were able to spin it around to expose the back of the file cabinet. I took out my handy jack knife and selected a screw driver head and began to loosen the screws on the back of the file cabinet. When I had finished Henry Stanton looked amazed. In the back of the cabinet were concealed several small objects and a small painting.

"You hired me to find your missing art. Here it is. How you want to proceed from here is your business. My guess is that Templeton needed some extra money when you cut back his hours. I'll be sending you my bill.

"Thank you Mr. Dance," Stanton stuttered as I left, though I wasn't sure he really meant it.

"It was in the file cabinet?" asked Judy in astonishment. I had only given out a very spare outline of the case, preserving the name of the museum and the people involved. I did, after all promise discretion.

"Yes. I think some people seem to give in to temptation."

"What was stolen?" asked Velda.

"I can't say, other than to say they were small items."

"We'll probably figure it out when we read it in the newspaper."

"You probably will," I responded. "If it gets in the newspaper." I had a feeling that it would all be handled quietly to save the museum's reputation. It wouldn't look good to donors if they realized that security there was a bit slipshod.

"So you've still got the bishop's murder to work on," said Judy. "Any leads there?"

"I'm going to check a few leads in the Midwest where the bishop lived. They seem to be some scandal that's been hushed up. I need to check that out."

"You're going to go out to Wisconsin?" asked Velda in mock horror.

"God, no. A few telegrams should be enough. Anyway, let's order lunch.

"Thanks to you, Roscoe, we have a lead in the Rogers's shooting," said Rob.

"Glad to help out," replied Roscoe modestly, but I could tell he was beaming with pride as he served us dinner.

"What lead?" I asked.

"I was able to track down some of Rogers's poker buddies. They all agreed that he said he was going to come into some big money."

"We already know that," I replied.

"Yes, but two of his buddies remember him saying that those bossy church bastards would get theirs. So either he was blackmailing the church or stealing from them."

"So let me get this straight," I said trying to piece it all together. "Rogers worked for the church, was either blackmailing someone, or stealing money, and was shot and killed?"

"That's right."

"So the murder of Bishop Campbell and the murder of Bill Rogers are most likely related."

"Yes," said Rob, "it does appear that way."

# Chapter 29

Aiden Brookfield and Thomas Masson were among the guests as Velda celebrated moving into her new house. The two real estate men had handled the sale and since it was for cash they were able to finish the transaction in less than a week.

Velda had barely had the new furniture delivered before she invited a group to her townhouse to celebrate.

She had borrowed Roscoe and Jimmy for the evening. Jimmy was busy preparing food in her half furnished kitchen. Roscoe was tending bar in the hallway. Myra Pennington was busy taking notes for her next society column.

"I thought that the editors had started to give you better news stories and sprung you from the society beat," I said as I offered her a martini.

"They have given me real assignments, but I still like to cover special events. If I didn't write a society story now and then, I wouldn't be invited to the best parties, and I do love a party. Where's Rob?"

"He'll be here," I said. "He's home changing. He just got off work."

"You look spiffy in your black tie and tails," said Judy Hogarth as she approached me. She was wearing a tight fitting blue evening gown with silver sequins. She seemed to shimmer as she walked.

"You look pretty spiffy yourself,' I replied.

"This old thing?" she laughed.

"I see," cut in Myra, "that Tommy Beckford is already acting the part of the boyfriend." We looked over to see Tommy escorting Velda around the room.

"Is it serious?" asked Myra.

"My sister and I are alike in one way," I began. "We are always serious about love."

The chatter and clinking of ice in glasses suddenly stopped and all eyes turned toward the door. Rob Williams had arrived in his black tie and tails and everyone stopped to look at him.

"I swear," said Myra. "The two of you should go to Hollywood. If you don't both outshine those Hollywood sissies, I don't know who could."

Rob took a drink from Roscoe and then headed over to our little group. "What are you three cooking up?" he asked.

"Love potions," laughed Myra and she grabbed Judy's arm and left us alone.

"You work too hard," I complained. "I hardly ever see you."

"You see me plenty," he replied. "I'm pretty certain I'm going to take the insurance job. It will give me more time to be with you."

"That would be lovely," I replied.

Velda and Tommy drifted over to us arm-in-arm.

"Who are all these people?" I asked. There were probably about thirty people in the house, and I could only name ten of them.

"Most of these are artist friends of mine," said Velda. Tommy Beckford was beaming at her.

"And a few of them are old college buddies of mine," Tommy added.

"Did you invite them for their looks?" I asked. Everyone in the room was young, good looking, and dressed to impress.

"They're all rather bohemian, wouldn't you say?" said Tommy as he finished his martini. "Anyone care for a refill?" Velda gave him her empty glass.

"He thinks this is bohemian?" remarked Rob when Tommy was out of ear shot.

"He's spent too much time in the Back Bay," said Velda. "I'll show him what bohemians are all about."

Velda had hired a small jazz band and when they were finished setting up they began to play. Several couples started dancing and Tommy and Velda joined them.

"Care to dance?" asked Rob taking my hand.

"You'll shock the sensibilities of the Boston Brahmans," I answered.

"To hell with them." Rob led me to the small section of bare floor that was being used for dancing.

"I forgot how well you dance," I told him. To everyone's credit no one gave us a second look.

"I doubt if this makes Myra's column." I noticed Myra and Judy holding hands in the corner and tapping their feet to the music. "I can see the headlines now: police detective caught dancing with another man in Beacon Hill raid."

The dance music stopped and trays of appetizers appeared. Maybe it was the bad economy, but the guests began to devour all the food in sight. Jimmy and Roscoe retreated to the kitchen to prepare the buffet.

The background music started up as people loaded their plates with food. The tinkling of ice in martini glasses was replaced with the sound of silverware clinking on china plates. There was the buzz of muted conversation that competed with the music. Rob and I filled our plates and then he motioned me to the kitchen.

The kitchen was a disaster area and Roscoe and Jimmy were working in the pantry. We sat at the small kitchen table.

"Something about the Rogers' case?" I asked.

"It seems that Rogers was a frequent customer of the bar you had closed down."

"So?"

"He was seen meeting with the same guy several times in the days just before the shooting."

"That doesn't mean anything."

"He was seen accepting a large wad of bills from this other guy."

"That does put a new spin on things. Did you get a description of the other guy?"

"Yes," said Rob. "But it was just a general description that would fit half of Boston."

"I can't help but think it has to be related to the bishop's death."

"That is a puzzle."

"What did you just say?"

"I said, 'it's a puzzle.'"

"That's what I thought you said."

I remembered the puzzle books amid the volumes of theology we found in the bishop's apartment. I remembered the half finished word jumble on his desk, and the list of words on the piece of paper we found in the bishop's prayer book.

"I know who killed the bishop," I announced to a startled looking Rob Williams.

# Chapter 30

R ob and I left the party a little after midnight. According to Velda the party went on until around three in the morning. Tommy Beckford got very drunk and passed out. All others seemed to have remained more or less sober. I was happy to have Velda back in my life and have her make a life in Boston.

Rob and I didn't talk about the case anymore that night, but over breakfast he began to question me.

"So you know who killed the bishop?"

"If my theory is correct yes."

"You'll need some solid evidence."

"How about the bishop telling us in writing?"

"What are you talking about?"

"Remember the piece of paper we found in the bishop's prayer book?"

"Yes, it was just a list of words."

"Remember the books on puzzles the bishop had in his apartment?"

"Yes."

"Those weren't just random words he wrote out, those were anagrams."

"Anagrams?"

"Yes, the letters are scrambled to make new words. The bishop may have left us a clue on purpose. He may have had some suspicion that he was in danger and left us a clue."

"Who is it?"

"I need to find that piece of paper again to be sure. But if I'm right, then we'll have a motive, and I'm pretty confident that we can tie it to the Rogers' murder too."

"That would be great, except I doubt if a word puzzle will excite the district attorney."

"I think we need a set up. One that will force a confession. For that I'll need your help."

"We are a team and you can always count on me."

"You can count on me, too," said Roscoe as he sat a fresh pot of coffee down for us.

I found the bishop's paper in my study and sat at my desk decoding the words. I was right! Everything fit. But could I get a confession?

It was time to make a few phone calls and set up a meeting. I rang the bell for Roscoe.

"Yes, Mr. Jeremy?" he said when he came into the room.

"Could you set up for a small group meeting tomorrow afternoon? Coffee, tea, that sort of thing?"

"You know I can."

"I know, just checking." He went away chuckling.

Before I attempted to reveal the killer, I thought it important to report to the people who were paying me. They should be the first to know.

I also invited Sister Mary from the convent since she was a good friend of the bishop. This was a formal meeting, and Rob was also attending to add the police perspective. Roscoe was dressed in a business suit in the role of my assistant. Sister Mary was the first to arrive.

"Thank you for coming sister," I said. "There have been some new developments in the death of your friend the bishop, and I thought you would like to be informed." I introduced her to Roscoe and Rob.

"That is most kind of you to invite me." I briefly explained that Bishop Anderson and his staff had hired me, and that they would be arriving shortly. "Have you arrested someone?" she asked Rob.

"No, sister. We don't have enough evidence yet."

"I hope whoever did it will be brought to justice."

The doorbell rang and Roscoe brought in Bishop Colin Anderson, Archdeacon Peter Ramsey, and Canon Tim Black.

"Thank you for coming," I said to the guests. "Please have a seat." Jimmy Kirk appeared with coffee and a tray of cookies. I waited until everyone was served, and we had all exchanged pleasantries before I began my report.

"This case has been a difficult one to say the least. There have been few clues and many obstacles. I'm afraid it has taken longer than I planned. I can't tell you how sorry I am that two of your staff have died in such violent ways. I thought I'd begin with just a brief review of the facts.

"The bishop's body was found outside of a private club in downtown Boston in the rear alley. The alley turns out to be a meeting place for several less savory characters. My first suspicion was that the bishop was a victim of a robbery gone wrong, or a random violent attack, or that he was involved in illicit activities himself.

"When lieutenant Williams and I went through the bishop's belongings we didn't find anything of note, except a paper with random words scribbled on it, but we did notice that his appointment book was missing. This, we figured was a major piece of evidence, but we couldn't find it.

"Other clues came to light only after I had to force the issues. Gentlemen, when you hire someone to look into something, it would be helpful to be open and upfront at the beginning. Your failure to do so ended up costing me time and you money. It also cost me a bump on the head from undercover work in the alley. That, too, will be reflected in the bill. Finally Tim Black told me about a scandal involving the bishop and his choir director at the cathedral in the Midwest. This lead was hard to follow up on because the church tries its best to avoid scandal. So here we have a motive for murder.

"Next Bishop Anderson confides in me that Bishop Campbell was working on finances for the diocese and that he had discovered that money was missing. So here we have another motive for murder.

"The first break in the case came with the discovery of the appointment book. It was found in the washroom of the private club that the bishop had visited prior to his death. But again this turned into a dead end. All it showed was that he met weekly with a SM, which turned out to be Sister Mary here.

Sister Mary nodded to the group. I continued.

"The words 'lamb tick' also appeared in the appointment book several times, but that made no sense to us. Finally we discovered that the bishop was meeting with someone at Gibby's Restaurant, which is just up the street from the Windsor Club. When we checked at the restaurant we learned that indeed the bishop had reserved a table for two, but that he had never made it to dinner that night, nor did we know with whom he was dining. This was another dead end.

"It was unlikely that we would ever learn who killed the bishop, but then there was a shooting at a downtown bar. The victim turned out to be a janitor who works for the diocese. I have to tell you that two untimely deaths in one small institution could not possibly be a coincidence.

However, there was nothing to tie the two deaths together."

"So are you saying, that Bill Rogers' death is related to the bishop's murder?" asked Colin Anderson.

"That's exactly what I was getting at."

"That seems most unlikely," said Tim Black.

"Then let me continue. Sister Mary, you knew Bishop Campbell better than anyone here, did he have any hobbies or interests?"

"Oh, yes," began Sister Mary. "He was quite fond of word games. He was great at crossword puzzles and word jumbles."

"I thought it strange when Lieutenant Williams and I went through the bishop's apartment and there among all his scholarly books were books on word puzzles."

"I don't see where this has anything to do with the murder," said Peter Ramsey.

"Yes," agreed the bishop, "I'm lost."

"It has everything to do with the bishop's death," I answered. "Because it was the bishop who told us who was guilty."

"What are you talking about?" interjected Tim Black.

"I'm talking about this," I said as I picked up the sheet of paper from my desk. "This is the paper that we found in the bishop's *Book of Common Prayer*." All eyes were riveted on the paper. I held it up for them to see the words were clearly written in a bold hand:

**Lamb Tick**

**Toles**

**Eco Sides**

**My One**

"At first," I continued, "the words meant nothing, but then I realized that they were anagrams." I could see the blank look on Peter Ramsey's face. "An anagram is a word made up of the letters of other words. You can think of it as a type of code. The bishop was very clever; he knew if anything happened to him the person responsible would go through his things and destroy anything incriminating. A list of random words would mean nothing at the time, but there was a chance that someone might figure it out."

"I'm still lost," admitted Bishop Anderson. What do the words mean?"

"I've rearranged the letters for you." I held up another piece of paper that I had worked on. It read:

**Tim Black**

**Stole**

**Diocese**

**Money**

All heads turned to look at Tim Black, but Tim Black was nowhere to be seen. Off in the hallway was the sound of a scuffle, and Roscoe and Rob returned with a defeated looking Tim Black in handcuffs.

213

"I'm arresting you for the murders of Bill Rogers and Bishop Angus Campbell," said Rob. Two police officers who had been stationed in the kitchen took Canon Tim Black to police headquarters to be booked.

# Chapter 31

Champaign glassed clinks as we toasted the success of our investigation at an impromptu dinner party. Rob and I invited Velda and Tommy, and Judy and Myra. The six of us were in a festive mood.

"I have an announcement to make," said Rob. "I'm proud to say I'm to become the newest resident of Beacon Hill."

"Are you finally giving up the pretext of having your own apartment?" asked Judy.

"Yes, it's such a waste of money," he replied.

"I'm sure there were other matters to consider," added Velda.

Rob smiled and looked at me, "Oh, yes, there were."

"I don't understand," said Velda getting back to our reason for the celebration, "how you figured out that the murder of the janitor was connected."

"It's a moot point now, because Black has confessed to both murders. It was Jeremy who made the connection."

"How did you figure it out, Jeremy?" asked Myra.

"The only description we had was that a man who was meeting Bill Rogers wore clothes that seemed too big for him. Other than that the descriptions of the man were unremarkable. When

I was meeting with the church people, I noticed that it looked like Tim Black had recently lost a lot of weight because his clothes were loose. Coupled that with the fact that Rogers worked for the diocese and was under the direct supervision of Black, it wasn't hard to make that leap."

"So how do the two murders figure together?" asked Judy.

"Bishop Campbell was investigating the disappearance of a good deal of church money." I explained. "The bishop figured out that Black was stealing the money, but I think he was trying to keep it quiet to avoid a scandal."

"According to Black's confession," added Rob. "The bishop made a deal with him. If he resigned and paid the money back, the police wouldn't be involved."

"He should have taken the deal," observed Velda.

"Apparently," I continued. "Rogers somehow got wind of the situation and started to blackmail Tim Black. That was his mistake."

"What will happen to Black now?" asked Tommy Beckford.

"He seems remorseful," answered Rob. "But most likely he will spend the rest of his life in prison."

"And I have one more announcement to make," I said. "It seems that Lieutenant Williams has decided to resign from the police department and work as an insurance investigator for Liberty Tree Insurance."

"A toast then to new beginnings," offered Tommy.

"To new beginnings," shouted everyone at once.

It was a quiet morning and I was typing out my report for Bishop Anderson when Roscoe entered the room.

"Lady to see you, Mr. Jeremy."

"Better send her in, Roscoe."

A tall woman whom I judged to be in her late thirties or early forties came in. She was dressed in a smart yellow suit in the latest style.

"I'm Jeremy Dance," I shook her hand. "And this is Mr. Jackson."

"I'm Martha Gilbert. Thank you for seeing me."

"What can I do for you, Miss Gilbert?"

"I need you to find someone for me."

"Tell me about it, Miss Gilbert."

"I have a brother named Ken. He joined the navy in 1932. Since then I've lost track of him. I want to find him, Mr. Dance."

"As it happens, Miss Gilbert, I'm taking a much needed vacation, but my business partner, Mr. Jackson here, might be willing to take the case. Mr. Jackson is an experienced investigator."

I thought Roscoe's eyes would pop out of his head when I called him my business partner.

But the truth is I could use some help. Roscoe managed to compose himself by the time she turned around to face him.

"Would you help me, Mr. Jackson," she pleaded.

"Yes, Miss Gilbert, I will."

Boston was hit with an early march snowstorm that left over a foot of new snow on Beacon Hill. Schools were cancelled, and transportation was difficult. The radio called it one of the worst March storms to hit New England.

I didn't care; I was sunning my naked body on the deck of an eighteen foot sailboat off the coast of Key West, Florida. I looked up to see a very tanned Rob Williams at the helm of the sailboat.

"Where are you taking me?" I said to him.

"For the next month," he answered. "Anywhere you want to go."

"That," I said, "sounds perfect."

## The End

Made in the USA
Lexington, KY
30 July 2012